A Time to Love
By
Kenya Henderson

First paperback edition December 2021

Book Cover by Rose Miller

ISBN 978=0-5788-5379-6 (paperback & ebook)

ISBN 979-8-7744-6552-1 (hardcover)

Published by Kenya Henderson

Acknowledgments

I'd like to thank my sister, Keena Nelson, for her encouragement, help, and advice. Many thanks to my friend Janna Morrison for allowing me to pick her brain to obtain information for this book. Thanks to my Aunt Johnnie Mae Fox for your financial support. I am grateful to my developmental editor, Aminah Paden, for her wisdom and expertise. Also, thanks to my spiritual father, my pastor Dr. W. L. Stafford, for his prayers and labor of love.

To the readers of this work, thank you for your interest in this story, which encourages forgiveness and love.

I've saved the best for last. To my Lord and Savior Jesus Christ, thank you for giving me the ability to create stories, which point to salvation, healing, and restoration. You provide whatever a person needs, and I thank you!

Table of Contents

Chapter 1

The evening sun began its slow descent. Light shone through the window, cascading across the coffee table, where a manila envelope held the paternity results. A bead of sweat rolled down David's face. He felt his heart thumping, as he picked up the envelope. Breathing deeply, he opened it and slowly withdrew the contents. Disappointment engulfed him, like a tidal wave of emotion. David sat down to gather himself with anger simmering just beneath the surface. Suddenly, his breathing became shallow and strained. His calm, poised demeanor shattered with a single teardrop, which flowed from his pain-filled eyes.

David was in his home office thinking about his wife of fifteen years. Jackie is the love of his life, and the betrayal cut him to his core. According to the paternity results, he is the biological father to only two of their five children. He'd known that Jackie wasn't happy for a long time. Nothing he did pleased her. However, not even his doubts and fears about the relationship brought him to this unimaginable conclusion that his wife is unfaithful.

Wiping away the last remnants of tears, he stood up and walked purposefully toward his desk. Picking up the phone to call his mother Deloris, he sat down in the lush, leather executive chair, where he normally felt in control. David began to dial. He pressed the numbers firmly and with determination.

"Hello," a friendly voice answered on the other end of the phone line.

"Mom, it's David," he said, choking back sobs from deep within him, which constricted his throat. He lifted his arm to brush away the sweat from his forehead, wiping his hand on the side of his fine linen suit pants leg.

"David, what's wrong," she asked?

"Do you think it's alright if the twins and I go to stay with your sister for a while," he asked.

"Of course, honey," Deloris responded, with concern evident in her voice. "You know that you and your children are always welcome at Aunt Gladys' house."

"Thank you so much," he said. "It's a last-minute trip, and we'll drive from here to Georgia tonight."

"I'll call Gladys," she said. "I'm sure she'll have the rooms ready when you arrive."

After finalizing arrangements with his mother and speaking with his Aunt Gladys, David felt a little better. He had a plan. His entire life, he'd always been methodical. Planning helped him to avoid the unexpected hurdles of life.

He looked out the window, watching a flock of birds flying south in a beautiful, multi-colored sunset. Exhaling a deep breath, he moved toward the front door, grabbing his car keys on the way. A faint scent of potpourri tickled his nostrils, reminding him that tonight he'd leave his home indefinitely. Despite its white pillars, hardwood floors, and smart home system, the beautiful interior trappings only reminded him of the ugliness of the situation confronting him. The sweet fragrance turned his stomach, causing him to vomit his lunch in the evergreen bushes, outside the mahogany double doors.

Wiping his mouth with a handkerchief, David walked a few feet to his midnight-black Mercury SUV. He heard the familiar beep of the door unlocking before entering the luxurious cream-colored interior and navigating the circular driveway. David said four words silently to himself before beginning the 20-mile trek to his mother-in-law's house to pick up his children.

"Lord, give me strength," David prayed.

Across town, Jackie looked across her mother Bernice's mid-century kitchen table into the faces of her children. The enticing aroma of soul food wafted through the air from a dinner meal of barbecue chicken, sweet potatoes, and greens. In the background, she heard the faint rustling of leaves on the trees outside the open window. A familiar repetitive dripping noise from her mother's sink was barely perceptible, drowned out by the voices of her children. They wanted to know why they couldn't go home.

"Why do we have to wait for dad," Nakita asked? "You know what happened," she continued, looking at her mother with expectation for an answer. David's twin brother Damon walked across the room to put his hand on Jackie's shoulder in a show of support.

The doorbell rang. Jackie's sister Jada yelled that she'd answer it.

"Alright, if you must know," Jackie sighed. She paused and looked each one of her children in the face. "Your father left me, because he no longer loves me."

Everyone yelled out an exclamation simultaneously.

"That's not true," Dana yelled!

"I don't believe it," Nakita shouted!

"No way," Junior wailed!

"Uh uh," Ashley cried out!

Dana immediately burst out in tears. Nakita sat at the table with her head down. "Mommy, are we going to see daddy again," Nakita sobbed into her mother's blouse?

"Of course, you will see your father again," Jackie hugged her oldest daughter.

"I hate this," Dana shouted, as she stood up from the table. "I hope he never returns!"

"Dana," Bernice commanded her attention, "don't you ever say that again!"

"Ahem," Jada interrupted Bernice, as she walked into the kitchen with David following closely behind her.

David's hard, angry look belied the pain he felt.

"Daddy, how could you," Nakita cried?

"I can't believe you don't love mom anymore, Dad," Dana shouted in anger and started to run upstairs.

Bernice grabbed her. "I told you to behave yourself," she said. "You don't know the whole story. Now sit there and listen!" Bernice looked pointedly at her daughter, "Jackie, tell these kids the truth."

"No, allow me," David offered curtly, walking closer to the table. "I heard what you said, Jackie. So that's how it is? You'll sit here and lie to them and make me look bad. How dumb do you think these kids are? You don't think they're going to figure out the truth? I guess it doesn't matter. I came here for my children."

"I'm not going anywhere with you," Dana snapped.

"Shut up, Dana," Bernice and Jada screamed in unison!

"I wasn't referring to you, Dana," David replied.

"Huh, well Dana is your daughter, and you agreed to let me keep them until tomorrow," Jackie said with an attitude.

Beneath the stony demeanor, David's heart thumped wildly. He looked around Bernice's kitchen for a moment, noting that Damon's eyes were glued to the floor. He'd learned a long time ago to count down from ten when he was angry to give himself time to process an appropriate response. 'Ten...nine...eight,' he thought to himself.

David looked at Jackie with disdain in his eyes. "I had the other children tested to find out if they were mine," he said. David looked down and shook his head. When he looked back up, he noted the surprise and fear on Jackie's face. Throwing the test results on the table, he continued, "I'm only the father of two."

"Are you serious," Jada interjected, as she grabbed the results off the table? "You're only the father of two?"

"Yeah, so the children you were going to leave with me, I'm leaving with you," David proclaimed to Jackie.

Junior looked confused.

"David, hold on there," his brother Damon implored.

"Man, don't you speak to me," David bellowed! "You run around here sleeping with my wife, and you think I'm going to raise your children," David asked?

"Not anymore, I'm not," he said. He looked at his wife, as he motioned to the twins.

"Junior and Nakita, get your stuff," David growled. "We're leaving."

Ashley and Dana were crying harder now.

At that moment, David realized how difficult it would be to leave the girls. He'd raised them as his own daughters. "Come on, let's go into the living room," he said to the children. "I'll explain everything to you."

Everyone got up to leave the kitchen. "You two stay put; you've caused enough damage," David barked, as he held out his forearm to block Jackie and Damon from coming in.

It was almost a relief to relax for a moment with his children. David eased into the soft pillows of the overstuffed sofa.

"Dad, what's going on," Dana asked, as tears rolled down her face? She didn't want them to leave her, and she was sorry for her disrespectful words.

"I want all of you to listen to me very carefully," he explained, looking the children in their eyes. "After your brother Tony's accident, he needed a blood transfusion. As you know, your mother and I were tested. She wasn't a blood-type match, and neither was I."

"What does that mean," Nakita asked?

David looked down at his hands, gathering his wits and strength to finish what he was about to reveal to the children. David sighed, "what it means is I'm not Tony's biological father. My brother Damon is his father."

Silence engulfed the room, as the children slowly realized the implications of his father's words.

"As for the rest of you, the DNA results show that I'm not Dana's father or Ashley's biological father either," David said, turning to the girls. "I'm not trying to abandon you, but your mother left me for Damon. I'm assuming Damon is your father."

Dana's face turned red, as the words hit her like a ton of bricks. Ashley sat shaking her head. Tears rolled down their faces, as sobs racked both of their bodies. David wrapped the girls in his arms, giving them time to process the news. Junior and Nakita joined the hug.

"Guys, we need to go," David said.

It was too much for him to bear. He gently released Dana and Ashley, stood up, and walked to the door. Tears welled up in his eyes. David didn't want the children to see him cry.

The twins ran upstairs to get their belongings. Dana moved closer to David, crying and pleading with him not to leave her. He kissed her softly on the forehead.

"I love you," he said. "You have a father who needs you, just as you need him."

Jackie and Damon came into the living room. "David, you can't leave Dana and Ashley."

"Oh yeah, Jackie," David mocked her in a monotone voice. "You sure were going to leave them with me. Remember that? You and Damon decided you were going to take Tony and leave me to raise the other children. Your plans have backfired on you."

"David, you wanted all of these kids. I begged you to stop when the first two were born, but you wanted this, not me," Jackie yelled!

"Well Jackie, you should have done the honorable thing and told me about you and Damon," David shouted. "Instead, you kept quiet and kept your legs open for him and for me!"

11

They both were screaming at the top of their lungs.

David realized that the argument was out of control. His mind went to the children, but he couldn't stop himself. His pain fueled the verbal assault, and Jackie was hurt. He'd never spoken to her so harshly. She pursed her lips, put her hand on her forehead, and walked away.

Damon stepped to David. "You didn't have to talk to her that way," he said quietly. "She is going to need time to adjust, and we are going to need the house."

"Negro, I 'm not giving you my house. Get your lazy tail up and get a job. You're going to need it now. Our sister Micki wants the house. If you want it, buy it from her."

"David, may I speak to you outside," Bernice asked? She wanted David to calm down.

"Bernice, I don't have time for this," he said. "I have to go."

The twins were coming down the stairs.

"Tell your grandmother, mother, and your sisters goodbye, because you won't see them for a while," David told his children.

The twins hugged Jackie. She held them closely. Guilt and remorse flooded her heart. David waited patiently, as the children hugged everyone. Then, the twins walked to the door, standing beside their father.

"Where are you taking them," Jackie inquired?

"Some place you're not going," David responded curtly.

Jackie held out her arms to hug them once more. They looked at her and then at David. David motioned for the twins to walk out the door. They left the tense atmosphere in the house, moving into the warm evening air. David quickly closed the screen door and speedily descended the four wooden stairs into the front yard, moving as fast as possible toward the truck.

Jackie called out to her children, the pain in her voice echoing into the neighborhood streets. Nakita kept walking to keep up with David's brisk pace, but Junior glanced back for a moment. His heartbeat quickened, with his emotions torn between love for his mother and pain from the family's separation.

Bernice sat in the living room to comfort Dana and Ashley; both felt the sting of rejection from the only father they'd ever known. Jackie and Jada watched David and the twins depart, until the car was no longer visible.

Damon came up from behind. He wrapped his arms around Jackie. She rested her head on his chest, and the familiar aroma of his aftershave relaxed her.

"Come on," he said softly. "We've got to go see Tony."

"Wait," she replied. "Let's just stand here for a moment."

Her family is torn apart, and the pain of it cut like a knife. The emotions heightened her senses. She could faintly hear jazz music coming from the neighbor's house. A slight breeze captured a fallen leaf, moving it across the yard. Jackie noticed the moonlight shining through the leaves from Bernice's mulberry tree, as the warm night air moved through the screen door. She sighed deeply, and her initial decision to entertain Damon's early advances played out in her mind's eye.

Chapter 2

Ten Years Ago…

Jackie's eyes blinked open to see David gazing at her lovingly. She smiled slightly and puckered her lips for a kiss. He complied, softly brushing her lips with his own. A warm feeling began to expand from the pit of Jackie's stomach, as the kiss deepened. The warm embrace didn't last long, as they heard a knock on the door. Nestled deep in the pillows and comforter, Jackie didn't want to move.

"I've got it," David whispered, kissing her ear softly before easing out of the bed into his slippers and walking toward the bedroom door. He turned the brass handle to open the door, just as Nakita and Dana started to walk away.

"Good morning, honey," David said.

"Hi, Daddy," Nakita replied. "What's for breakfast?"

"Is that all I get for a morning greeting," David inquired playfully, scooping the girls up into a hug and tickling their tiny bodies, until they fell to the floor laughing uncontrollably?

"Well, I'm hungry," Dana replied through her laughter, holding tightly to the arm of her favorite brown teddy bear.

"Me too," Junior piped in, walking toward them from his room at the end of the corridor.

"I think the children need some cooking lessons," David taunted. "What do you think wifey?"

"It couldn't hurt," Jackie chuckled, smiling as she slipped into her robe. "David, if you bathe them, I'll have breakfast ready in about thirty minutes."

"Aye, Aye Captain," David saluted and tucked each girl in his arms to carry them toward the hallway bathroom. Junior laughed at the funny expressions on his father's face. The girls giggled. Just then, Ashley cried from her crib.

Jackie heard David running bath water for the children and quickly pulled the sheets up, making the bed. She walked toward the master bathroom, removing her night gown and dropping it into the clothes bin. Jackie looked into the mirror. Her eyes were sad. She had everything that she'd ever wanted, a loving husband and beautiful family. Her hands ran across her stomach as to rub her unborn baby. Yet, she longed to control her own destiny. As she quietly reflected on her life choices, Jackie turned the knob and hot water from the shower began fogging up the mirror.

Stepping into the shower's water, Jackie wished she could wash away her thoughts of Damon. David's twin brother was always around, spending time with the family. Lately, the hugs that she and Damon shared were lingering a little longer than usual. There was a longing between them. She couldn't quite pinpoint when things had changed, but she didn't want to cause problems between David and his brother by mentioning it to her husband.

She would see Damon today, when the family came to visit the house after church. She was excited about the thought of hugging his muscular physique. Closing her eyes, she thought of him as she washed.

Jackie caught herself, diverting her thoughts back to David. She moved out of the shower, put on casual attire to cook in, and walked down the stairs to prepare breakfast for her family.

"Hmm, something smells good," David whispered in her ear, as he touched the small of her back and kissed her gingerly on the cheek. The children followed their father into the kitchen, walking to the table to sit down. Sunlight flooded the breakfast nook through a large bay window, reflecting off the fine cut glass dishes, as gospel music filled the room.

At the table, the family held hands, bowing their heads to pray.

"Father, we thank you," David prayed. *"Thank you for this meal we are gratefully receiving, for the love of family, and for your grace. Amen."*

In the present...

David pulled up in his driveway. He got out of the car, and the children followed. The twins were reluctant to speak to him. He had a look on his face they'd never seen. It was a scary, intimidating look. Neither of them wanted to bear the brunt of his frustrations.

Nakita and Junior walked through the front door, surprised at all the boxes cluttering the foyer. David sat down on the couch, placing his elbows on his legs and his face in his hands. He felt a sense of relief at retrieving the twins without incident, but the emotional pain was unbearable.

The children looked at each other. They didn't know what to do. Junior sat down across from his dad. He was furious at his mother and uncle.

Nakita stood there looking at all the boxes. She walked into the kitchen and saw boxes all over.

"I had the family come over and pack up the house, while you were gone," he explained.

"Why Daddy," Nakita asked, sitting next to her father?

David took a deep breath, his eyes darting to the left as he explained everything to them from the moment he found out about Tony until now. They'd heard some of the story, but he wanted to help his children understand.

"So, you knew mom was cheating on you and you didn't tell us," Junior muttered. He was already hurt by his mother's actions. He couldn't believe his dad kept that information from them.

"Yes, I didn't want to tell you, until after Tony was out of intensive care," David explained.

"So, Dana, Ashley, and Tony are our cousins and siblings?" Nakita was trying to wrap her head around everything.

David nodded his head in agreement, saying "I'm afraid so sweetheart."

"That's messed up, Dad," Nakita responded.

"Yeah, how are we supposed to explain that to anybody" Junior lamented? "Things like that happened on television, not in real life."

Nakita cried, "why would mom do that to us, huh Dad?"

"I don't know," David said, his face crestfallen.

A text message came to his phone. It was his sister Micki, wanting to know the paternity results. David text her the results, knowing Micki would spread the information to the entire family.

Sadness engulfed David, as he grabbed Nakita in a hug, reaching out his arm for Junior to join. The three of them wept bitterly. In that moment, David decided that he had to be strong for the children.

"Hey, let's stop crying," David implored. "We are going on a road trip."

"Really," Nakita sniffed.

"Cool," Junior replied, wiping away his tears.

David couldn't wait to leave this home, which was filled with memories of Jackie and Damon.

Ten Years Ago...

It was time for Sunday dinner and the family was having their weekly gathering at David and Jackie's home. The festivities start around noon. It was a potluck gathering. Each family member chose a dish to bring, ensuring the feast would be enough to feed everyone.

Deloris thought of her three sons. She was concerned about Damon, who was still finding his way in life. Chris is well off with his doctorate degree in mathematics, but his faith wavered from time to time. David had it all together. Dedicating his life to God at a young age, he always met challenges and successes with the same measured response. He called his parents, Deloris and Joseph regularly to check in and offer help, as needed.

Deloris heard Micki suck her teeth. She looked up and saw Damon walking toward them. It was a hot day in July. Everyone was shocked to see him. Damon was noncommittal, so no one ever knew when he'd show up.

The children were playing frozen tag and stopped when they noticed Uncle Damon. Deloris motioned for them to continue playing.

"Damon, you decided to come," she hugged her youngest son.

"Hi Ma," Damon said, bending down to hug her. Deloris leaned into him and put her arms around him.

Jackie spoke up from an adjacent card table. "How are you doing, Damon," she asked? She had a smile on her face.

Joseph walked over and embraced Damon. He said a quick, silent prayer, *'Lord, please give my family a beautiful day to fellowship with one another, strength to accept our differences, and enough love to treat each other as family.'*

Micki has been known to speak bluntly, especially to those who have disappointed her. Joseph prayed that the family had a good time, and his daughter didn't give anyone a tongue lashing.

It was a scorching hot day. If it weren't for the shade from the majestic oak trees and bags of ice, it would be unbearable. Still, everyone enjoyed themselves while fellowshipping and eating. Laughter filled the air, as the family played volleyball, Uno, and Bid Whist.

David sat on the bench in the corner, leaning forward with his face in his hands. He hadn't eaten anything yet, and his mind kept wandering back to Jackie. He looked across the yard to find her.

His mother Deloris came and stood near him. "I see you're over here all alone thinking about your wife," she smiled, as he looked at her embarrassed that his love for his wife was still so obvious after five years of marriage.

David gave her a half smile. "I don't know how you know me so well, Mom," David said. He took his mother by the hand and gave her a peck on the cheek, as she sat down by him.

"I remember you telling me that you had to convince her to marry you."

He was surprised that she brought that up. "Yes, she was reluctant because of what her parents went through."

"Is that what she told you," Deloris asked?

"Yes, well I don't know," David sighed. "She said she wasn't ready, but I assumed it had to do with her feelings about her parents' divorce." David stared down at the ground.

"What else did she tell you," Deloris prodded?

David's eyebrows came together, and his lips poked out a little. "What do you mean," he retorted?

Deloris thought about it for a minute. She wanted to choose her words carefully. "I recall a time when Jackie didn't want any more children after the twins were born," she explained. "She said she expressed to you that two children were enough."

"Why are you bringing this up now," David asked his mother?

"No, what I'm saying is that you need to listen to her even when you don't like what she is telling you," Deloris replied.

"Okay, Mom," David responded.

"I consider her feelings," he explained. "Everything she's ever wanted I gave her. She doesn't have to ask or want for anything. Sometimes, it takes me a while to get what she wants, but I get it for her all the same."

Deloris gave him a sad smile. "I'm not talking about material things, sweetheart," she said softly. "What I'm asking you is can you consider her requests? Why you Campbell men don't listen to anyone else is beyond me. Shouldn't what she wants be a factor in your lives together," she said, leaning her head to the side and pursing her lips.

David scowled briefly. "Thank you for your advice, Mom," he replied, taking her by the hand to guide her to dance in the grass to the beat of the music in front of his family.

"I let her stay home from work after the twins were born, so that she wouldn't have a reason to complain about working and taking care of a family," David continued the conversation, as they danced.

"Do you hear yourself," Deloris inquired of her son with compassion?

David was at a loss. Deep down inside he knew his mother was right. He did force Jackie to comply with what he wanted. Even though he wanted a lot of children with her, she didn't want a lot of children.

"I understand what you're saying, Mom," David chuckled. "Jackie often says, 'you never want to do what I want'.

Deloris reached out and hugged her son, hoping that he listened to her, before it was too late.

David nodded his head and smiled. He thought back to the day Jackie brought him home to meet her family. Bernice pulled him to the side and informed him that her daughter was sneaky and conniving. She always wanted her way and would pout if she didn't get it. Her exact words floated back through his mind, like she'd said them yesterday. "I know your family is upstanding," Bernice told him. "So, I know you're an upstanding man, and I'm not going to lie to you. You can do a lot better than my daughter."

David shared what happened that day for the first time with his mother, as they danced. He'd kept it to himself all these years. Jackie didn't even know her mother told him not to marry her. He didn't know why the words suddenly came to his mind. As he danced, he looked around the yard for his wife.

Inside the house, his brother Damon pulled Jackie closer. She settled into the hug, her arms reaching around his chiseled frame. Her senses picked up the faint scent of mouthwash mixed with an enticing cologne aroma. He held her longer than he should have, but Jackie couldn't bring herself to break the embrace.

Damon looked around, noting that they were alone. He took her hand, guiding her downstairs into the family recreation room. Walking through the colorful décor, they entered the laundry room. Hoisting Jackie on the washing machine, Damon teased her lips with his tongue, pulling her against him. She trembled and sighed. It felt good, and she didn't want him to stop. Damon continued, pulling her panties aside underneath the summer skirt that she wore. She grabbed the back of his neck and bit her lip to keep from screaming his name. In the distance, she heard the family's laughter and music. Damon kissed her deeply, moving her from the washing machine to the floor. She closed her eyes, as she tried to not let the guilt ruin the overwhelming sensations she felt.

Chapter 3

In the present...

The harsh reality of his failed marriage hit David hard. His aunt's house would be a welcome retreat from the emotional turmoil of the past week. After packing, David loaded the twins into the car and drove south on I-75. As he drove, he thought about the events that had taken place in his life, the good and the bad. Who would have ever thought that things would turn out the way they did? He knew his brother was foul, but he didn't think he was that low down to sleep with his wife. It didn't just happen once, and they left each other alone. They slept together for years. He was still having a hard time accepting that the other three were not his children.

David remembered the day he and Jackie first met. For him, it was love at first sight. She stood in front of him with her perfect figure. Her beautiful, long, and curly hair cascaded down her back. She wore a chic, tan skirt and a pink blouse. Even her White Diamonds perfume enticed his senses, wafting through the air and drawing him to her.

It never occurred to David that Damon also loved her all those years. She seemed like she was into David, but it was fake. He can remember times when she professed her love for him. It melted his heart, when she agreed to marry him. He felt like the luckiest man alive. She was beautiful on the outside, but there was no way he could ever take her back now.

Nakita and David Jr. were concerned about their father. He had a blank expression on his face, the same as when he picked them up from Grandmother Bernice's house. He wasn't driving recklessly, but he wasn't talking either. They sat in the back whispering to one another.

"Where are we going," Nakita asked David Jr.?

Junior shrugged his shoulders, replying "maybe you should ask dad."

Nakita's brows came together. "I'm not going to ask him," she said. "You ask him."

Junior refused, believing his dad was less likely to snap, if Nakita asked him a question. "He likes you more."

"That's not true; don't even try it," she whispered.

Finally, the twins decided on rock, paper, scissors, and Nakita lost.

She took a deep breath before inquiring, "Dad, where are we going?"

David looked at her through the rearview mirror. "Atlanta, sweetie," he replied. He heard his children in the back seat quietly whispering, but his mind was on Jackie. David's thoughts went back to their wedding day. The church was packed with family and friends. There were twelve bridesmaids, all dressed in beautiful maroon, which is Jackie's favorite color. Damon was his best man, and David invited some friends from college to be groomsmen.

He could still see her standing down the long isle at the entrance to the sanctuary on her father's arm. Jackie wore a veil to cover her face. The dress was white with pastel-colored sequins on the bodice and a long, removable sweep train hooked to the dress. David sang the song, Love Ballad by L.T.D., as she walked down the aisle. The church had maroon seats, so the colors matched perfectly.

After the ceremony, they transitioned to the reception hall at the local UAW. Everyone partied until two o'clock in the morning, laughing, eating, and dancing. Their families knew how to celebrate a wedding big time. He began to smile, as he thought about it.

David instinctively reached for Jackie's hand, but she wasn't next to him in the car. The sad reality hit him again. His bride was in the arms of his brother. She'd broken their wedding vows in the worst possible way. David's anger welled up within him again. Before he knew it, the car's speed increased to eighty-five miles per hour in a seventy-mile zone.

He heard the siren before looking into the rearview mirror at a fast-approaching state police vehicle.

David sighed and shook his head. After he pulled over, he leaned his head back on the head rest.

"Dad," Nakita said anxiously.

Junior was also nervous.

"It's ok honey," David explained. "I was just speeding while thinking about your mother." He exhaled loudly, as he waited for the officer to write him a ticket.

After receiving the ticket, David continued driving south toward his aunt's home. The twins fell asleep in the back seat. Before he knew it, they were in Kentucky. He kept driving. A lot of thoughts ran through his mind. His thoughts turned to the children he left behind. Jackie couldn't care for them on her own. He already knew Damon would be little to no help. His brother never held down a job for more than a year, and most of them were low-income jobs. It wasn't fair to the children.

All of this could have been avoided if Jackie and Damon would have come clean. They had no right to keep their love affair a secret from him. Word has it that they had no intentions of letting him know what they had been doing for so long. What kind of woman would do such a thing? And what kind of brother was Damon? David started to get angry all over again. He felt himself speeding down I-75 and heard a voice within telling him to slow down. He needed a rest. David pulled off the highway onto Man O' War Blvd in Lexington, KY to find a hotel.

They lodged in a room with two queen-size beds. David Jr. wanted pizza for dinner, so they ordered from their favorite pizza place. Everyone sat quietly, waiting for dinner to arrive. Nakita and Junior were extremely concerned for their father. He's never been this distraught.

David sat at the foot of the bed on the edge. He was leaning forward, his face in his hands. His elbows rested on the knees, as he contemplated his next move. Almost overnight, his whole life turned upside down. His wife left him for his twin brother, and three children that he raised from birth did not belong to him. Defeat rose up in him. *'Where did I go wrong,'* he asked himself? *'That woman never loved me.'* All the negative emotions he'd felt before resurfaced. He was about to pound his fist on his leg, when he heard his daughter's voice.

"Dad, do you know where to go," she spoke timidly to her father?

"Yes, I know how to get to Aunt Gladys' house," he replied softly.

Gladys Hicks was Deloris' youngest sister who'd moved to the Metro Atlanta area years ago. She was dark skinned and a little on the heavy side. His aunt always enjoyed visits. She kept the family laughing, and it was fun being around her.

According to his family, Aunt Gladys' children didn't like them much. Deloris was lighter than her sister, and Gladys always felt that her parents cared more for Deloris because of her skin complexion. David didn't care about relative dynamics. They were family, and he always made it a point to visit them.

As David contemplated his decision to leave Michigan, he decided to make the move a permanent one. The twins would have to transfer to the schools down south, because he couldn't bring himself to return. Everything in him went dark, whenever he thought of going back. There was nothing left there for him besides his family. Not even his family could help him overcome the emotional turmoil from more than ten years of deception in his marriage.

25

He decided that once they reached his aunt's house, he'd make arrangements to transfer the twins to a local school and request a job transfer from Michigan to Georgia.

As he continued the long journey to Atlanta with his children, David couldn't help remembering the phone call he received just one week ago, which shattered his marriage, split up his family, and sent his life into a tailspin.

One week ago...

David's cell phone rang. The phone was tucked away in his suit jacket pocket. When he answered the call, he heard someone crying and screaming but could not make out what they were saying. He didn't look at who was calling, because he couldn't take his eyes off the road. Jackie was sitting in the seat next to him, and she could hear someone on the other end screaming as well.

"What," David exclaimed! "I can't understand what you're saying." He passed the phone to Jackie. "I... I don't know who it is or what they are saying."

Jackie noticed from the caller preview screen that it was Dana. "What's wrong, Dana," she asked? "He did what! Oh my God, is he alright," she inquired? "Ok, we're on our way, we're on our way!"

David could hear the frantic tone of her voice. "What happened," he asked anxiously?

Jackie started crying, tears streaming down her face. David pulled the car over, so he could find out what was happening. Jackie shook her head no, "we have to get to the hospital," she replied. "Tony ran out into the street and was hit by a speeding car."

The blood in David's face began to drain. "Is he alright," he asked, as he reentered traffic?

All she could do was shrug her shoulders.

"Dana says it looks bad," Jackie answered. "Please hurry." They were leaving downtown Detroit and had to go to West Bloomfield, a little over 30 miles away. David stepped on the gas and prayed they were not stopped by the police.

By the time they arrived at the hospital, his older brother Chris and his family, his parents, and Jackie's parents were already there. The police were there as well talking to their children. David and Jackie ran straight to the emergency room desk.

"We're here to check on our son Anthony Campbell," David explained, while he attempted to calm his emotions. The last time the family experienced a tragedy is when his brother Derrick was killed by his wife a little over three years ago.

"I'll call the doctor for you," the nurse offered.

David's mother walked up to him. "I've called Bishop Hayes and the prayer warriors," she explained. "It's going to be alright son, because God has it all under control."

"How can you say that," Jackie wondered out loud, as tears began to stream down her face again? "How can you possibly say, 'He has it under control'" Jackie repeated? "Where was God when my son got hit?"

David reached out to hug her, but she pushed him away. "This is all your fault," she shouted! "If we had stayed home, our son would not have been out in the street."

"Why are you blaming me," David exclaimed? "I don't know why he was out in the street after dark, but I'm definitely going to find out."

Jackie's mother Bernice spoke just then. "Jackie, you can't blame him," she contradicted her daughter! "Wasn't Damon watching the children?"

"That's what I want to know," David's mother interjected.

Bernice reached out for her daughter. Jackie was crying uncontrollably now. Dana walked up to her mother and wrapped her arms around her from the back.

Jackie's mother Bernice was petite, standing a little over 5 feet and 4 inches, the same height as Jackie. Her fair complexion was smooth, covered by expertly applied foundation and makeup. Bernice was meticulous about her appearance, and even in an emergency trip to

27

the hospital, every hair on her head was in place, showcasing her old-school, bob hairstyle.

"Daddy," 14-year-old Nikita spoke. "Is Tony going to be alright?" Her sweet, innocent voice melted his heart, as he comforted her before attempting to find out the answer to her question.

Suddenly, Damon rushed into the emergency room. David walked up to him and grabbed him by his collar. "Where were you," David yelled? "What happened and why was my son outside?" Before he could contain himself, his hands moved toward Damon's neck, until his father-in-law's intervention stopped him.

Jackie's father Charles Eldridge Sr. stepped between Damon and David, as their parents Joseph and Deloris comforted Dana, Ashley, and the twins.

Damon described the events of the evening, explaining why he was outside with them. They'd decided to play hide and seek in the dark to make it more fun. He said that he told the children not to play in the street. Unfortunately, Tony didn't listen and ran into the street before Damon could catch him.

The family looked at Damon, as if he'd lost his mind.

"You did what," Joseph asked with his lips compressed? His eyes bore into Damon like a snake ready to snatch his prey.

The rest of the family gasped in shock at Damon's negligence.

"I didn't know he would go into the street," Damon said apologetically. "I'm sorry y'all!"

"I can't believe what I'm hearing," David exclaimed. "Lord, help us...God didn't give you the sense of a turnip." He shook his head as Damon continued to talk.

"I swear none of this was supposed to happen," exclaimed Damon. "I just wanted to have some fun with the children." He was in tears and kept talking, but it was muffled because of the sobs.

"Mr. and Mrs. Campbell," Dr. Montgomery called to them, as he walked into the emergency room. Stretching out his arm to shake both their hands, he simultaneously motioned for them to follow him. "Let's go somewhere and talk privately." He led the way to his office. As they entered, he pointed to the two chairs as a gesture for them to sit down.

According to the doctor, Tony suffered injuries to his lower abdomen and part of his skin was ripped open when the vehicle hit him. "He's lost a lot of blood from the injuries," the doctor continued. "He'll need a blood transfusion."

"We're willing to get tested for a blood match." Jackie spoke before the doctor could finish his statement.

David nodded in agreement.

Doctor Montgomery smiled. "All right then, let's set that up," he replied. "If you're both his biological parents, then one of you should be a match."

"I'll need you to sign some consent forms, and then we'll head to the lab," he said. "Also, since your son suffers from seizures, I'm keeping him in a medically induced coma until the transfusion and the pain from his wound isn't so uncomfortable."

Dr. Montgomery had worked with Tony in the past, and was familiar with his medical history and condition. David and Jackie were relieved to finally have a plan to help their son.

The family was on edge, as they waited for an update. Tony's grandparents Deloris and Joseph, were praying in the corner of the hospital waiting room.

Micki entered the room, after a run to the vending machine. She was Deloris' niece, but she raised her as her own daughter. Micki was loud, boisterous, and bold. She didn't care how she spoke her mind, because getting her point across was all that mattered to her. She was very outspoken about the amount of time Jackie and Damon spent together, and she didn't care much for either of them. She tried to show compassion to Damon, because he is her brother. Jackie and Micki always had some word exchanges, whenever the family came together. She did not hesitate to let Jackie know how she felt about her in general.

Micki spotted her parents in the corner praying. The girls and Junior ran up to their aunt Micki to get some snacks. Dana and Ashley were still crying. Junior had a blank look on his face, and Nakita held on to her aunt for dear life.

"Has the doctor said anything", Micki asked, looking expectantly at all four of them for a response?

"The doctor took mom and dad to his office to talk about Tony," Nakita cried. "I can't stand all this waiting."

Micki reached out and hugged her again. "It's just the usual procedure," she said. "The parents are usually the first to know anything, and then the rest of the family will get word." She looked up and saw her parents walking toward them.

Micki hugged both Deloris and Joseph before offering them some chips and candy from the vending machine. "Do you have an update on Tony's status," she asked?

They both shook their heads. No one knew why the doctor took them to his office. Deloris explained the injuries Tony experienced to her daughter.

"How did he get hit," Micki exclaimed? "I don't understand why he was outside so late."

Both of her parents put up their hands as if to surrender. "All we know is that Damon was playing hide and seek with the children outside in the dark," Deloris explained. "He claims he told them not to go in the street, but Tony didn't listen to him."

"The young guy that was driving the car was speeding," Joseph said. "Ain't this a mess?" Deloris nodded her head in agreement.

Micki turned to her nieces and nephew. "Why in the world would you play hide and seek in the dark," she asked? "That doesn't make any sense."

"We were just trying to have some fun," Dana responded. She was trying to make light of the fact that they were outside well after 9 p.m. Her parents never let them stay outside that late to play.

"Haven't you ever played outside after dark, Aunt Micki?" Junior questioned his aunt, trying to ease the tension. He loved Uncle Damon and didn't want the family to bad mouth him.

Micki sighed, "Well, I guess I have, with Mom and Dad watching us, of course." Looking around she asked. "Where is that bone-head brother of mine?"

"He stormed out of here, after David jumped on him," Joseph explained, describing to Micki what happened. "You would think these boys didn't have any home training the way they were carrying on."

They both looked out the window to see if he was in view. Since Micki didn't see him when she arrived, she and Joseph decided to go look for him.

Her father suggested that she not criticize him for his decision. He was just trying to pass the time and entertain the children while their parents were away. He understood what his son was trying to do. At the same time, it's dangerous outside. Even though Damon was outside with them, anything could have happened, and it did. You don't hear much about crime going on in Bloomfield Hills, but you cannot be too careful.

They exited the emergency room doors and headed to the right. Damon was walking toward them and talking on the phone to someone. When he spotted them, he informed the person he was talking to that he would call them back. Damon approached Micki and Joseph with a look of frustration on his face.

"Son why don't you come on back into the emergency room," Joseph said?

Damon shook his head. "I'm not going back in there," he replied. "I'm going to leave and come back when David is not around."

Micki held up her hand to stop him from storming off. "Do you think that's wise," she asked? "I know what happened between you two, but the children will expect you to stay with the family."

He smirked and stared at her. "I don't think it's good for me to be with the family right now." Damon replied. "I am very pissed at David, and I could strangle him for what he just did."

Joseph tried to calm the anger that was growing inside him. Damon does make a lot of stupid decisions, but David has always taken up for him. Even though one of David's children is hurt, he still loves Damon. Joseph was convinced of that fact.

Damon shook his head as he walked away. He entered his car, a black Ford Mustang. Joseph and Micki stood on the sidewalk watching as the car left the hospital grounds.

"Well so much for that," Micki stated. "It's like talking to a brick wall. He's done more dirt than any of us put together, but no one is supposed to tick him off." She kept on rambling, until she saw the look on her father's face, that made her shut up. She looked down at the ground and followed Joseph as he turned to go back inside.

By the time Micki and Joseph returned, David and Jackie were back in the emergency room. David was filling the family in on Tony's condition. Micki could tell that Jackie was upset with David. She wasn't standing close to him. Jackie was looking out the window, probably wondering where Damon had gone. She turned to speak with Micki about Damon. Micki gave her a look, which said don't even think about asking. Jackie turned back to the window with her arms folded across her midsection.

"We thank everyone for coming out to check on our son," David said to the family. He encouraged them all to go home and get some rest, promising to fill them all in once they received the information about the blood transfusion. Everyone was reluctant to leave, but he assured them it was best.

Jackie wanted to change into something more comfortable, and she wanted to find Damon. She left with her mother and said that she would be back as soon as she could. David knew better. His wife didn't handle tragedies well.

Walking slowly toward the intensive care unit, a wave of guilt washed over David. He wished he could have protected his son from this accident. A throbbing pain made its way from the pit of his stomach and into his chest, as he entered his son's hospital room. Kneeling by Tony's bed, he prayed over the thin, broken body of his youngest child.

Several hours later, Dr. Montgomery returned. He motioned for David to follow him into the hallway. Cafeteria workers were distributing breakfast to the rooms. David could smell the distinct aroma of eggs, as he entered the hallway. Looking at him directly in his eyes, the doctor told David that neither he, nor Jackie were blood matches for their son, Tony. In the background, David heard a beeping noise from a machine in a nearby room. He noticed one fluorescent light bulb was not working down the hallway. In the quiet bustle of the intensive care unit, David felt all alone, when he realized Tony was not his son. He asked the doctor to run the test a second time. It was shocking news and hard to believe. He had to be sure.

In the present...

Memories of the past continued to haunt David, as the sound from his mobile phone ringing brought him back to the long ride to his aunt's house with the twins. He answered the call, speaking through the Bluetooth device in his ear, "Hello."

It was Aunt Gladys. "I'm just checking on you and the twins," she said. Her comforting, jovial voice brought a smile to David's face.

"We are close," he replied, putting her on speaker so Nakita and Junior could hear the conversation. "Say good morning to your aunt," David prompted them.

"Good morning, Aunt Gladys," the twins replied in unison.

"Hi, my darlings," she exclaimed. "We are so excited that you are coming to see us!"

Even with everything that happened, David couldn't help but feel a sense of excitement at the prospect of starting over in a new area. "We're excited, too," he responded.

"I spoke with Deloris," Aunt Gladys continued. "She said Tony is much better and should be home in a few days.

"Good," David replied. The pain of losing three of the children that he thought were his was still very raw. He quickly changed the subject. "We should arrive in about six hours, Aunt Gladys."

"I'll let your uncle know that you are halfway," she said. "Drive safely and love you all."

"Love you too, Auntie," the twins responded.

When he disconnected the call, the emotions from the past week welled up within David. He stopped to order the twins breakfast from a local restaurant, before continuing the journey. Aunt Gladys' update about Tony was good news. It was also painful, because it reminded him of the situation that he left back in Michigan. As he drove, the twins fell asleep. Junior's soft snore was the only sound in the silence of the vehicle. David's mind wandered back to Tony and his time with him in the intensive care unit.

Chapter 4

One week ago...

Deloris walked into Tony's hospital room in the intensive care unit the next morning. She saw David silently praying. He sat with his eyes closed, head bowed, and the movement of his lips barely perceptible. She sat in the other vacant chair, causing David's eyes to open. She didn't want to leave her son and grandson at the hospital alone. She and Joseph agreed that she should return to keep David company.

As she looked around the room, an indescribable feeling came over her. Tony was fighting for his life, hooked up to machines, and breathing into a clear oxygen cup over his mouth. He was stable, but anything could go wrong.

Her daughter-in-law blames David for Tony's accident. It seems that the relationship between Jackie and David was on rocky ground. That didn't sit right with her. She wondered if David noticed. The rest of the family sure did. When she came out of her reverie, David was staring at her with a smile.

"Oh, I'm sorry to disturb your praying," Deloris said. "How are you doing son?"

He sighed, "for the most part, I'm ok...I'm believing God that He will heal my son." If only for a moment, he wanted to hold onto this child he loved and cherished. Emotions welled up in him, as he looked at Tony's limp body.

"I'm so sorry you're going through this son," Deloris offered words of compassion, which was just what David needed.

David smiled, as he looked down. "I can't believe this is happening," he said, referring to both the accident and its aftermath. "You hear about children being hit by cars on the news or see it on social media, but I never expected it to happen to my child."

"I shouldn't have grabbed Damon like I did," he continued with a hint of depression in his voice. "Jackie blames me for all of this."

"I'm sure Damon will forgive you, and Jackie will come to her senses soon," Deloris interjected. She rose from her chair and walked over to her son to gently rub his back. David was thankful for his mother who always had a way of easing his burdens.

They sat in silence, both silently praying to the Lord for Tony's healing. The nurse walked in to check the vitals. His condition hadn't changed. He needed a blood transfusion.

Jackie walked in right after the nurse left. David walked toward her. "Jackie, we need to talk," he said. She held up her hand.

"Don't touch me, and don't talk to me," she replied. "I'm still incredibly angry with you, and I'm just here to check on my baby."

Deloris got up to leave. "I'll be in the waiting room." She gave her son a reassuring smile, as she walked out.

"Jackie, we need to talk," David repeated.

She gave him a fiery look. "It's because of you that we're even in this mess," she exclaimed!

"Lower your voice for goodness' sake," David motioned toward Tony, as if he's worried that the arguing would wake him up.

Jackie closed her eyes and took a deep breath before responding again. "If you had listened to me, we would have been at home and the children would not have been outside."

She walked over to Tony and kissed his forehead. Jackie grabbed a chair and pulled it toward her son. She took Tony's hand and sat down in the chair beside his bed.

David's hurt and anger began to swell within him. He breathed deeply in and out, maintaining control of his emotions.

Jackie's heart raced, as her blood drained from her. "If you'd only listened to me," she said. "I don't like being controlled all the time."

"Don't you dare try to make me the villain," David retorted, easing toward the doorway to move the escalating conversation away from Tony.

"Look, I just want to be here for Tony," she cried. "Please don't say anything else to me."

"The house is vacant," she continued. "So, you can go home if you want."

"What do you mean the house is vacant," David asked in confusion?

"I mean I've moved in with my mother, until this ordeal is over," Jackie replied.

"What are you going to do when Tony's recovered," he questioned?

"We'll discuss that later," she said. "Right now, I want to spend time with my boy."

David stood there contemplating what to do next. His wife just told him that she'd left home. David's entire world was collapsing around him, and he tried to figure out how it all happened. He didn't understand Jackie's reasoning, because he'd always given her everything she'd ever wanted. However, he didn't want to have an argument in front of Tony, even though the boy was still in an induced coma. So, David walked away, taking with him his hopes and dreams for the future of his family, which he'd carefully planned and crafted over the years.

Jackie was glad David left the room. *All of this could have been avoided if he'd just done what I asked,* she thought to herself, as she held Tony's hand. Now what was she going to do? Her faith in God wasn't as strong as she portrayed. She really didn't believe in God as much as her husband. David was the spiritual one of the two. Her family didn't raise her in the church, as her husband's family did him. They attended on Resurrection Sunday, Mother's Day, and Father's Day, if her parents wanted to go. Sometimes, they would go on Christmas morning. Ever since she met David, she's been in church every Sunday. Church and family gatherings were the major reasons she and David were still together.

David's mother cooked or the entire extended family got together for a potluck meal every Sunday. All of them gathered after church to fellowship, but family members had to attend service to eat dinner. The Campbell family seems like the only family around that keeps that old tradition alive. She would endure a few hours in church to avoid slaving in the kitchen. Unfortunately, now her relationship with her husband was broken. She was tired and ready for a change.

Jackie looked down at her son. Her young child was fighting for his life. *How could this have happened,* she wondered quietly to herself?

"I'm sorry Tony," Jackie spoke to him, as tears began to run down her cheeks. A mother is supposed to protect her children, and she'd failed miserably. "I should've stayed home, sweetie," she said. "You wouldn't be here now, if I had." Jackie knew he couldn't hear it, but she had to voice what she was thinking.

Her mind wandered to the day Tony was born. She'd caught a glimpse of his tiny head in the mirror above her, as she gathered all the energy within herself for one last push to bring him into this world. When she held him, his tiny eyes opened for the first time, curiously looking around. Full of energy, the baby quickly grew into an energetic toddler. Even at his young age, Tony was always thinking of inventive ways to bring the family together. Jackie smiled to herself, as she thought of her boy.

There was so much going on in her mind. She's heartbroken over her son, and she was in an unhappy marriage. Suddenly, she wished her father Charles was here. He was a good listener and always knew what to say to make her feel better.

The nurse walked in to check Tony's vitals. Jackie took a deep breath, as the nurse checked his blood pressure and temperature. She was a young African American of dark complexion, probably fresh out of college. She didn't look any older than twenty-five. The nurse smiled at Jackie when she was done. "I'm believing God will pull your son through this," she offered Jackie a half smile before leaving the room.

Jackie was baffled, because even the nurse had faith in God. She sighed. "Everyone's believing you'll pull through, baby," she spoke to Tony. "I'm hoping you will." She bent over the rail to kiss his forehead, while maintaining a gentle grip on his hand.

Releasing the grip, she went out to the nurse's station to get a blanket. At one point, Jackie wanted to see if her husband was still around. David was still Tony's father and deserved as much time with him as he wanted. After much contemplation, she decided to stay in the room by herself. One of the chairs in his room was a recliner. Jackie laid back in the chair and tried to think happy thoughts, as she drifted off to sleep.

David woke up in the intensive care unit's waiting room with his family all around. His father was back, along with his sister, Micki and brother Chris with his wife and children. They were still eating breakfast that they must have purchased, before they arrived. He spoke to everyone and thanked them for coming, as he stood and stretched.

Dr. Montgomery came into the room. He wasn't expecting all the family members to be present. He walked in to speak with David. "Mr. Campbell, I need to speak to you in my office," he said. "Please follow me."

David figured Dr. Montgomery had received results he requested. Still, he asked about Tony, "Is my son ok?"

"Oh, there's been no change in Tony." He gave him a half smile, but a worried look as well.

David followed Dr. Montgomery to his office.

"Please have a seat, Mr. Campbell."

"Doc, what's going on?" David sat down in the chair Dr. Montgomery offered him. He was nervous.

"We need a decision about the blood transfusion," the doctor replied. "Should we supply blood from the blood bank, or do you want to test other family members?" He looked at David and waited for a response.

David's eyebrows came close together. "Is there any way that you could have made a mistake," David asked? "I am his biological father."

Dr. Montgomery shook his head, and he took a deep breath. "I'm afraid not," he said. "You and your wife were not a match for Tony, so there's no way you're that boy's father."

David's heart rate quickened, and he jumped out of the chair. "I am his father," David exclaimed, as his grief took on the stage of disbelief! He started throwing a lot of questions at the doctor.

"I'm sorry Mr. Campbell," he said, removing his glasses and rubbing his eyes in exhaustion. "DNA doesn't lie. I've ordered the test twice just as you've asked. I'll have to have a donor to match Tony, before we can do the blood transfusion. I know this comes as a shock to you. However, for Tony's sake, we have to test other family members or choose a match from the blood bank."

David couldn't hear what the doctor was saying. His mind started racing. As he walked out the door, tears began to run down his face. This couldn't be happening to him. He'd done everything right. He prayed daily, took care of his wife and children. Had God forsaken him?

David entered the waiting room and sat down. He was crying uncontrollably now. The family gathered around trying to comfort him.

"What happened," Joseph asked, as the family crowded around David. "Is Tony alright?"

He was trying to speak, but he couldn't get control of himself. "Tony's not...," he couldn't seem to muster enough strength to say the words. He was still crying, and his speech was a little muffled. He tried again. "Tony's not...," he uttered. He was rocking and crying with his hands on his face. "Tony, Tony," he cried while shaking his head.

Dr. Montgomery walked in. Deloris ran up to him. "Dr. Montgomery, what happened," she wailed?

"Tony's fine everyone, and he's still stable," the doctor replied. "I'll let Mr. Campbell fill you in on the details, while I go check on Tony in the meantime." Dr. Montgomery knew that David had a hard time accepting what he told him. He stepped in the waiting room on purpose to reassure the family that Tony was fine.

"Ok, if Tony's not dead, then what's the problem," Micki asked, looking at David? "Come on, brother, what's wrong?" She knelt in front of him.

He was starting to hyperventilate, while praying at the same time.

"The Lord is my shepherd...," David prayed.

"Someone, please tell us what is going on," Micki repeated impatiently. Something was wrong with her brother, and she wanted to get to the bottom of it.

"Micki, stop it please," Deloris scolded Micki for her impatience.

When David gathered himself, he was able to speak. Tears were still running down his face, but he was doing much better than before. "Tony's not my son." There, it was said. He really didn't want to say anything, but his feet directed him to the waiting room after the doctor confirmed the results that he'd given him earlier. He looked up at everybody and repeated the words, "Tony's not my son."

Everyone was in shock. Micki spoke up first. "I knew it," she proclaimed.

"You knew what," her father asked?

"I knew that trick was cheating on him," she muttered. Chris and his wife, Trina, exchanged a surprised look at each other.

"Oh Micki, not in front of the children," Deloris didn't want her grandchildren to hear the family bad mouth Jackie.

"Mama please, they've heard that word before," Micki responded.

"David son, I'm sorry." Joseph sat down next to him, placing a hand on his arm.

David sucked his teeth and shook his head. "I can't believe she did this to me," he asserted. "I've been there for her, her mama, her brothers, and her spoiled sister. He stopped speaking, not wanting to bring the image of his wife sleeping with another man to his mind.

"Is she still here," Micki asked, just as Jackie walked in? "I'm going to give her a piece of my mind."

Instead, David jumped up and confronted Jackie. He no longer felt constrained, since they were not near Tony. "You cheated on me," he accused her. "How could you do this to me?"

"I trusted you," he exclaimed. "I've been there for you and you treat me like this!" David's voice rose above the volume of the television in the corner of the room. Everyone in proximity heard the exchange.

"David, lower your voice," his mother admonished him. People were coming into the room and staring at them.

Joseph grabbed his son to pull him away from Jackie. David went willingly. He couldn't stand to look at her.

"What are you talking about?" Jackie looked confused, even though internally she knew that David spoke the truth.

"Oh, don't play innocent," Micki blurted out! "You know exactly what he's talking about, and your skanky tail needs to tell us who the father is so Tony can get a blood transfusion."

42

Micki was in Jackie's face, ready to come to blows.

Ignoring Micki's instigation, Jackie addressed her husband. "David, I need to talk to you," she said.

"Don't say nothing else to me," David replied. "You need to contact Tony's father, so your son won't die."

"Well, it would be your fault." Jackie said adamantly, still sticking to the idea that none of this would have happened, if they'd just stayed home the night before, as she wanted to do. In her mind, the entire situation was the result of a domino effect from years of David ignoring the things that she wanted for their family.

Micki did not buy into her delusions. "No, it's your fault, trick," she exclaimed, pointing an accusatory finger at Jackie! "You know you had another man all up inside of you, and you're trying to play like you did nothing wrong."

"I never liked you, Jackie," Micki admitted. "I saw you for what you really were, a lowdown, dirty, nasty, hoe."

Deloris moved in front of Micki and motioned for her to stop. But, Micki continued, "Now, my brother loves you to life, and you played him like a plum fool. Tell us who the father is, because I know you know, hoe." Micki started taking off her earrings and her shoes, preparing to jump on her sister-in-law in the middle of the waiting room.

"Micki what are you doing," Deloris uttered in disbelief?

"I'm going to kick her tail, if she doesn't speak up," Micki bellowed. Who is Tony's father, trick?"

"I'll call him," Jackie conceded, pulling out her cell phone and walking away from the waiting room.

"You'll call him," Micki and Chris repeated in surprise. "Ain't this about a ..."

Deloris interrupted Micki, before she could finish her statement.

Meanwhile, Joseph spoke comforting words to David. A child he'd raised since birth was in grave condition. He finds out he's not the father, and his wife committed adultery. That was a hard pill to swallow. The family was in shock at what they'd just heard.

Jackie walked back in the waiting room. "He's on his way," she explained.

David's facial expression reflected hurt and anger. "Who is it," he asked her?

She couldn't look him in the eye, keeping her head down, and refusing to respond to the question. "He'll be here, and you'll see," she said before running out of the room.

"Well, I think we've all had enough…," Chris gathered his wife and four children, preparing to take them home.

"No, don't leave, we need to confirm who this man is," Micki said. "Young lady this is too much for these children," Joseph replied.

He nodded in David's direction, "they don't need to see a fight, if the situation gets out of hand."

Chris decided at that moment that he will stick around just in case violence did break out.

Micki smacked her lips. "We all know who the Daddy is," she asserted. "Why is everyone acting so dumbfounded all of a sudden?" She couldn't believe her family didn't have a clue, or maybe they didn't want to accuse another family member without proof.

"This isn't something the children need to hear," Deloris agreed with Joseph.

"They're going to find out sooner or later," Micki responded, in a nonchalant tone. "Might as well let them find out now."

"Mom and dad are right," David agreed, embarrassed that his nieces and nephew had heard too much already. "The children don't need to be here," He went to the window, watching as Trina escorted them to her car. He wondered to himself, if he should test the paternity of his other children.

Chapter 5

Most of the family waited patiently to learn the identity of Tony's father. David kept pacing and shaking his head. Periodically, he mumbled something under his breath. Micki went off about how Jackie was evil and mean. She called her just about every derogatory name in her memory bank. Micki also paced back and forth like a lioness waiting to pounce on her prey.

Jackie sat outside of the hospital waiting for Tony's father. She knew it was wrong to blame David. She was tired of living a lie and should have left the marriage instead of cheating. Her heart belongs to another, and it was time to let go.

Looking across the main parking lot, she noticed a group of pigeons eating crumbs someone left on the ground. She noticed families coming and going. Medical personnel were walking in and out of the building, wearing their colorful scrubs.

Sitting alone, Jackie had time to reflect on her circumstances. There was no easy way to transition to a full-time relationship with her lover. The family would be devastated, because the children loved their father. David was a good provider to all of them, but he did not give her the mental and emotional stimulation that she needed. She hasn't wanted him for a long time. They argued constantly for years. Most of the time, they discussed problems in the car to keep the children from hearing them.

The children's welfare is the highest priority. Jackie wanted to wait until after Tony was well enough, before she told him about his real father. A wrong decision could impede her son's recovery.

Leaving David would crush her husband to the core. He deserved better, but she couldn't give him everything that he wanted. He wasn't a bad man, but he had high expectations for his family. Every time she fell short of David's expectations or ruined his carefully crafted plan for her life, she felt more self-esteem leave her. Happiness in the marriage didn't exist, so she tried loving the two men at the same time. Unfortunately, Jackie's heart drifted closer to her lover every day.

She didn't know what to do about it. Following her heart sounded like the logical thing to do. She'd followed her head for 15 years, and she was miserable. In her mind, David was the best choice. He had a career as an engineer and made well over six figures. Her husband also had businesses on the side, which increased his income. Financially, David is rock solid, even putting money away for their golden years and the children's college education.

So, who wouldn't want a man like that? She didn't, that's who. It baffled her, because this was the lifestyle she dreamed about when the thought of getting married came to mind as a child. Jackie could have whatever she wanted and not have to work for it. David let her work as a stay-at-home mom after the twins were born. She obtained her nursing degree and was working as a RN, when she left the career world.

It took a lot of patience to rely completely on her husband. She lost her independence when they married, and in some ways lost herself. With her lover, there is a freedom that she rarely felt with David. His carefree approach to life, gave her a glimpse of what was possible in a relationship.

Her mind drifted back to her son who was fighting for his life. This might be bad timing to break this news to her loved ones. Everyone is upset about Tony being hit. Her infidelity revelation would complicate things even more, but as the saying goes 'a happy wife, a happy life'. She wasn't happy and deserved to be happy after bearing five children.

Jackie and her lover talked about what they would do with the children. He hasn't said if they would keep any or all of them. It wasn't fair to divide them, unless David agrees to do so. It probably would be better to leave the children with David, until the two of them got on their feet. She thought about doing a six-month split. They would reside in the same area, so they wouldn't have to pull the children out of their school.

She saw Tony's father pull into the parking lot. His black vehicle parked just a few feet from her near the hospital entrance. As he stepped out of the vehicle, the sight of his tanned, muscular body gave Jackie butterflies in the pit of her stomach.

Revealing the truth to her husband's family was going to be difficult for everyone, but there was no turning back. It's out in the open now. Tony doesn't belong to David. The man that she loves is her son's father.

She stood up, as he drew near, and they embraced. Jackie took a deep breath. "Are you ready," she asked him?

He shook his head. "Are you sure we're doing the right thing," he asked her nervously? A lot of things could go wrong. What if Jackie's husband attacked him? Would children be in the vicinity? All kinds of thoughts ran through his mind.

"What are you talking about," Jackie inquired, confused by his hesitance? "We've waited and waited for this for a long time, so don't chicken out on me." She didn't care who disapproved. She was all good, if she had the man whom she loved by her side.

Tony's father knew that Jackie wasn't thinking clearly. Anyone in their right mind would see that this was a bad idea. He wasn't ready to reveal his identity to the family, but his son needed him and there was no turning back.

Jackie walked into the waiting room with Tony's father behind her. They stood in the middle of the room, staring at David. For a moment, silence engulfed the room. A muscle in David's neck twitched, as he tried to process this new information. He heard his heart beating wildly. Pain like none he'd ever experienced felt like a weight on his chest.

"I knew it," Micki proclaimed. "Damon's the father. I told y'all she was doing him. I knew it! I knew it! I knew it! I can't believe you would stoop so low, Damon," she continued. "This is your brother, your twin brother. How could you do such an awful thing?" Expletives began to leave Micki's mouth, like machine gun bullets at target practice. She called Damon every dirty word she could think of, before Deloris intervened.

Just as the last curse word left Micki's mouth, David's fist landed on Damon's left jaw. Micki's tirade had distracted Damon, and he never saw David coming toward him. He felt the full brunt of the punch, as the impact of David's fist pushed his inner cheek against his teeth, cutting him. He fell to the ground, with David towering over him.

Jackie quickly moved out of the way. Micki was yelling for David to kick Damon's behind. Suddenly, Damon and David were hitting each other in the face. David felt the jab to his eye, and a burning anger erupted in him. He knocked Damon to the ground again, hitting him repeatedly.

"You slept with my wife," David shouted. "You're a low-down, dirty bastard!"

Damon was still on the ground when David lifted his foot to stomp on him. Jackie screamed again and ran over to Damon. "Stop please," she implored, her voice reaching a high pitch, which echoed throughout the waiting room area!

Deloris reached her son just in time to prevent him from literally stomping his brother into the ground. David moved away from Damon and Jackie, giving them a withering look, which was filled with anger and pain. He wanted to continue and thought about attacking Jackie too. His fist balled tightly, David sat down on a waiting room chair near the windows.

For a moment, the only noise he could hear was the faint sound of rain that began to hit the windows outside the hospital. His brother's voice reached him, as the pain of betrayal took hold of his body.

David fell to his knees sobbing in front of his family and the crowd of strangers who had gathered in the waiting room area.

"I'm sorry, David," Damon said. "It wasn't supposed to go this far."

Deloris was shaking her head. "Damon, how could you," she cried? Tears rolled down her face, as she attempted to comfort David.

"Man, what has gotten into you," Chris exclaimed, his look of utter shock hurt Damon's heart.

Joseph, couldn't believe what he was seeing, closing his eyes for a moment of prayer. Damon had struck again, his actions causing a rift in David's marriage.

"Like I said, I'm sorry," Damon repeated. "If Tony is my son, then I'm going to take care of him."

Bloomfield Hills police department officers walked into the waiting area with hospital security personnel. The orderly pointed to Damon and David. "Those are the two who were fighting," the orderly said.

Hospital security officers told the police to remove them from the premises. "I would like these two men arrested," one security officer commanded, as she spoke into a radio attached to her shoulder to update the security office on the status of the fight.

"No please, I need him to donate blood, because our son needs a blood transfusion and...," Jackie said.

One of the officers stopped her midsentence, saying "I'm sorry ma'am, but these two will be arrested."

One officer grabbed David.

Dr. Montgomery came into the waiting room area. "What's going on," he asked the security guard?

"These two were in here fighting," the guard responded. "We do not tolerate violence here at the hospital."

"Alan, can I speak to you for a second," the doctor motioned for the security guard to follow him?

"I know these two have caused a ruckus, but one of those men is the father of a patient of mine," Dr. Montgomery explained. "He needs a blood transfusion as soon as possible."

Alan sighed and walked back into the waiting room to speak with the officers. After speaking with the officers, they escorted the twin brothers into Dr. Montgomery's office. Damon gave his blood for Tony's transfusion, before the brothers were both hauled off to jail.

In the present...

Atlanta, Georgia

The memories of the past week were too painful to revisit. David focused on driving through the suburban neighborhood just outside of Atlanta where Aunt Gladys lived. He was physically and emotionally drained by the time he pulled into the driveway. Gently waking the twins, David looked up to see his aunt and uncle coming out of the house toward the car. The twins ran toward them for a hug. David's eyes welled up, but he held back the tears of relief.

"Thank you, Father," he prayed silently.

Chapter 6

In the present...

Detroit, Michigan

Bernice sat at her kitchen table with a cup of coffee in front of her. Deep in thought, she barely noticed the pungent aroma, which filled her nostrils when she took a sip. She wondered what really happened between Jackie and David. Why was her daughter moving into her home? Her daughter had not mentioned anything going wrong with her marriage. She had so many questions she needed Jackie to answer.

For a long while, it was just Bernice and her daughter Jada living together. Now, her oldest daughter and her granddaughters Dana and Ashley are in her home. Jackie told her that when the hospital releases Tony, he'd move in too. She didn't want Jackie to give up on David, because he was a good husband. She had to get to the root of the problem to help her daughter figure it out.

Jada walked into the kitchen, interrupting Bernice's thoughts, as she plopped down into the chair across from her. She let out a long sigh, playing with her long, curly hair with one hand, while she strummed her fingers on the table with the other. "How long are Jackie and the girls staying here," Jada asked, with a tone of defeat evident in her voice? Bernice's youngest daughter often vented her frustrations, when Jackie stayed longer than a few hours at Bernice's house with her children. So, Jada was definitely not on board with a long-term living arrangement with her sister.

Bernice was agitated by her daughter's question. "I don't know Jada," she snapped at her.

Jada smacked her lips and stood up to get a drink of orange juice. "Well, they're getting on my nerves," she said, as she took the juice carafe out of the refrigerator, a tiny bead of condensation rolled down the exterior of the glass. "I don't have any peace, and they keep asking me about David. What am I supposed to tell them?"

"How about the truth, that you have no idea," Bernice's eyebrows lifted, as her daughter sat down across from her again.

"Well, that wouldn't be the truth, because we know all about Jackie and Damon," Jada had always speculated that her sister had been intimate with Damon, but never had real proof till the other evening.

"You think you know what is going on, but you don't know for sure," Bernice sighed. "Please don't talk about the affair to the girls, because it's painful enough for them already."

Jada stared at her mother in disbelief. *Was her mother crazy or in denial,* she asked herself?

"You can't be serious," Jada exclaimed!

"Jada why are you always borrowing trouble," Bernice responded. She didn't want to discuss it any further, especially with Dana and Ashley around.

"Mom please, you know Jackie messed up the marriage with that good man," she said. "It's obvious, isn't it?"

Just before Bernice could respond, she heard someone coming down the stairs. The girls were showered, dressed, and wanted to see their brother.

"Can we go see Tony now," Ashley pleaded?

"I'm sorry, that's not possible at the moment," Bernice replied apologetically. She felt bad for her granddaughters, knowing they wanted to connect with the only brother left in Michigan.

"Well can we at least go to the hospital, when mom goes this morning," Dana asked? "I'm sure she'll want us with her for support." She didn't mention Damon's name, because she did not think of him as her father.

"I think that's a good idea," Jada agreed, jumping up from her seat.

"That's not a good idea," Bernice interjected. "You will just have to stay put while your parents are at the hospital."

Disappointment hit Dana in the gut, and she lowered her head. Ashley began to whine.

Bernice tried to reassure her granddaughters and encouraged them to keep praying for Tony. It was hard to tell them no, but she and Deloris were texting last night. Everyone agreed that it was best to keep the girls away from the hospital.

Jada offered to drop Dana and Ashley off at a friend's house to give her mother a chance to speak with her sister. Bernice and Jackie were home alone, and Damon was on his way to pick her up. She wanted to talk to both Jackie and Damon together to find out how they were planning on living and taking care of the three children.

Bernice contemplated the best way to bring up the subject with her daughter and Damon. He had already shown signs of abandonment. Bernice knew that it was only a matter of time, before he dumped Jackie all together. She was angry with herself for not stepping in sooner. All the warning signs were there that Jackie and Damon were having an affair.

She lived through a similar situation, with an affair ruining her marriage to Jackie's father. It seemed inevitable that her daughter was on track to suffer the same fate. Unfortunately, Jackie is not using good sense. She believes Damon will be an upstanding man. Bernice feared that her daughter was in for a rude awakening.

Tears began to slide down her face, as Bernice thought of her grandchildren. This entire situation is going to be difficult for them, but she'd already made up in her mind that she was not taking care of them. The children belong to Jackie and Damon. *They will have to learn to act responsibly*, she thought.

The knock at the door broke her out of her reverie. She opened the front door to see Damon's chiseled, good looks. He smiled a half smile, but his eyes were sad. He stepped out of the humid, summer air into the cool air conditioning of Bernice's home. She couldn't help feeling uncomfortable with Damon. Tension filled the air, as he kept his eyes on the ground, refusing to look at Bernice.

Bernice pointed for Damon to go into the kitchen, and she called Jackie down to join them. When Jackie reached the kitchen, she paused when she saw Damon. They greeted each other with a comforting hug, before sitting at the kitchen table with Bernice.

Jackie sat next to Damon and wrapped her right arm around his left arm. Bernice sat there looking at the two of them. She could tell that neither one of them had a plan on how to fix the situation. Bernice had to light a fire under them, so that they didn't drag their feet. Jackie is a known procrastinator, and if Bernice didn't say anything, her daughter would be sitting at this same spot in the kitchen next year.

She cleared her throat. "I brought you two together to find out what's your game plan," Bernice said quietly.

They both raised their heads in her direction and looked at her in disgust.

Damon sucked his teeth. "Do we have to discuss this now," he asked, with irritation in his voice?

Bernice tilted her head to the right, maintaining a serious facial expression. "Yes, we do," she responded. "You two do not have time to sulk, because three children are depending on you."

Jackie and Damon tried to respond at the same time, but Bernice held up her hand to silence them.

A look of concern crossed Jackie's face, she looked around the room, and asked her mother about the girls. She didn't want her daughters to hear the conversation.

Bernice interrupted, "They're at a friend's house."

"It's just the three of us," she continued. "We are going to come up with a plan today."

"What's the rush, Mama," Jackie argued? Her nose crinkled, as a look of annoyance passed across her face.

"Well, as I've already told you," Bernice replied. "I'm not raising any more children."

"I don't think either of us is in the right frame of mind to discuss this right now," Jackie muttered, as she stood up from the table.

"I'm afraid you don't have a choice," Bernice insisted. "You both are going to need to find jobs to take care of your expenses."

Jackie stood there with her mouth opened. "What are you saying," she asked, sitting back in her seat?

Bernice bowed her head down. She wanted to explain to them how much she empathized with them, but she didn't.

"Damon, I know your siblings and parents are not going to raise these children for you," she told him. "You may have help from them financially, but I won't be able to help in that regard."

Damon folded his arms, sat back in his chair, and turned his head away from Bernice. Jackie had a confused look on her face. She began to shake her head, as her mother's words sank in. This wasn't the time. Tony is scheduled to come home in a few days.

Damon spoke after a few moments passed by. "Are you saying that we're going to be solely responsible for the welfare of these children," he responded?

"That's exactly what I'm saying," Bernice replied. "You all created this mess…"

Jackie broke into her mother's speech. "What do you mean, we created this mess," she uttered?

"You had unprotected sex with your brother-in-law and had these babies," Bernice responded quietly, but firmly.

"I didn't want all those children," Jackie explained. "David did."

Bernice leaned forward in her chair. "Well, if you had enough sense to have your boyfriend here wear a condom, you wouldn't have had all these children," said Bernice, thinking that her daughter had some nerve to blame David for children, which weren't even his.

Jackie was taken aback at her mother's reproach, but her mother was right. She and Damon should have used a condom.

Bernice spoke again. "I'm selling the house and moving into something smaller," she declared. "I want to travel, while I can still move around without any help."

"Why don't you just give the house to us," Damon asked haughtily? He was annoyed with Bernice, Jackie, and himself.

Bernice shook her head. "There's a mortgage on it and your brother and Jackie's father were helping me pay the bill," she replied. "If you want to purchase it, you are more than welcome to buy it." Bernice had a grin on her face.

They both scoffed. "You know what I mean Bernice," Damon responded. "We can take over the payments."

Bernice snickered. "I don't think so," she said, thinking to herself, *you're not going to get over on me with your good looks.*

"You will not ruin my credit, if you don't pay up," she exclaimed. "Put your own name on the line, if you want a house for your family."

"So, what are we supposed to do, Mama," Jackie sobbed? The reality of her situation was slowly dawning on her. She thought that her mother would help her, but she was mistaken.

"That's what we're here to figure out," Bernice replied, feeling sympathy for her daughter. "I'm sure you are going to have to take some classes to get back into nursing."

Jackie did not want to go back to work. She expected her life to remain somewhat the same. Only this time, she would be with the man she loved.

"I'm sorry, Bernice, but my mind is not focused right now," Damon responded by shaking his head. "All of these bombshells are dropping down all at once."

"First, we find out that we have three children together, plus you're telling us no one is willing to help us financially," he continued. "What are we supposed to do?" Damon pushed away from the table and stood with his hands in his pockets, staring out the patio door.

Bernice took a deep breath. "I don't want to keep bringing up what you did, but in all honesty and fairness, you should have thought of that before now," she replied. "It never occurred to either of you that you may be the father of these children, instead of David?"

"He was never supposed to find out, Mama," Jackie responded.

"You were going to keep this from him for the rest of his life," Bernice inquired in surprise? "That's just pitiful," her voice rose above the quiet, non-judgmental tone, which she had planned to maintain for the entire conversation.

"I didn't want to hurt him," Jackie explained. "I just didn't know how to tell him, so we agreed to keep it to ourselves."

"How is that working for you," Bernice asked sarcastically? She got up from the table. "You have three months to get your own place."

"What if I can't find anything in that time," Jackie asked, wringing her hands anxiously?

Bernice thought for a moment. "In that case, I guess you'll have to put the children up for adoption, if you can't take care of them." She left the kitchen abruptly and went to her room, leaving Jackie and Damon alone.

Tears began to well up in her eyes, as Damon came to her side and embraced her. The warmth of his body gave her comfort, while she reflected on the accident last week.

She was still angry with David for wanting his way all the time. If she'd only stayed home that night, Tony wouldn't have been outside to get hurt. Jackie heard the birds chirping outside of Bernice's kitchen window. The memories of the past week haunted her, like a bad dream that she couldn't forget.

Chapter 7

Last week…

Jackie was so disgusted with herself for not following her first mind. She had an uneasy feeling about the night the whole time. "I don't know why I didn't stay home," she complained, sitting in the passenger side of her mom's comfortable, modern sedan, as they drove home from the hospital. "I should've put my foot down, when I told David that I didn't want to go," Jackie exclaimed!

"Honey, there's no way you could have known what was going to happen. You leave the children with Damon all the time. You and David go out every third Friday of the month. Why should this time have been any different?" Bernice looked at her daughter with compassion.

"This doesn't make any sense. This is David's fault. I told him that we shouldn't go out every month on the same day, every third Friday. What's wrong with going on a Saturday or even on the second Friday of the month?" She kept ranting and raving, as her mother drove them home.

"Oh sweetie, you can't blame your husband…," Bernice cautioned her.

Jackie put up her hands to stop her mother. "If he'd listened to me Mama, we wouldn't be in this mess! He never does what I suggest or say. It's always about him and what he wants. We could've stayed home and watched a family movie or something. If he wanted it to just be him and I, we could have sent the kids somewhere. Instead, David insisted that we go out, even though I didn't want to do so," Jackie started crying again, as she complained.

"Mama, please stop," Nakita begged, pleading with her mother.

Jackie held her head in her hands. "I'm sorry, baby doll," she told her daughter calmly. "I'm just frustrated, and I don't know what to do."

"Mama, is Tony going to be alright," David Jr. asked?

Jackie looked at her oldest son with uncertainty. "I believe so," she replied. "Your father or I will give blood for his transfusion." She was more fearful than ever, because she hated giving blood.

Finally, Bernice's car made it back to David and Jackie's house. They found Damon sitting on the porch step with his head in his hands. "What's Damon doing here," Bernice asked her daughter?

"Children, please go grab some clothes and toiletries to take to your grandmother's place," Bernice said to Dana, Ashley, and the twins.

"Mama, we won't be long," Nakita replied, as Jackie opened the door, letting the four children into the house.

Jackie walked over to Damon. They embraced each other.

"I'm sorry I ran out," Damon said. "David made me so mad, and I couldn't take it anymore!"

"I know," Jackie replied. "He was wrong."

"How's my Tony man doing," Damon wondered, sticking his hands in his pockets?

"He needs a blood transfusion, as you know," Jackie explained. "He's stable right now. They're waiting on the results to find out which one of us is a match. I'm going to stay at my mother's place, until this is all over. I don't want to be around David at this time."

Damon nodded his head with understanding. "Are you going back to the hospital?"

She sighed, "yes, as soon as I shower and get out of this God-awful dress."

"You want me to stay here and take care of the children?"

"No, I'm leaving them with my mother," Jackie informed him. "I'm getting ready to pack some clothes for myself." She forced a smile, as she maneuvered around Damon to enter the house.

Bernice called Damon over to her car. "My daughter is a little confused on who's responsible," she told him, as he walked up to her. "She's actually blaming David for all of this."

"Yes," Damon responded. "She told me."

"Maybe the shock has troubled her brain cells or something," Bernice joked, as she looked at Damon pointedly, "Everything will be back to normal, after Tony is home and in good health. Just wait, you'll see."

Damon stared off into the sky, noting the constellations were clearly visible. He stood by the car for a moment and walked away. He knew that Bernice was making a point. He opened the door and sat in his vehicle to avoid any possible confrontation with Jackie's mother.

Bernice moved her car to let Damon out of the driveway, but he didn't move. So, she sat in her car waiting for her daughter and grandchildren. She didn't believe her daughter would be dumb enough to have an affair with Damon. Yet, the two of them appeared to be awfully close. She's warned her daughter about getting too close to Damon. It's bound to lead to trouble. She's asked Jackie many times about their relationship. Her daughter assured her that it was strictly platonic and family oriented. Yet, it just didn't make any sense to her that Jackie blamed her husband for Tony's accident. Damon was the adult in charge at the time.

She hoped her daughter wasn't committing adultery. David was a good husband and father. Well, Bernice thought to herself, *What's done in the darkness will come out into the light.*

An affair with Damon would devastate the entire Campbell family, as well as David and Jackie's children. Maybe David will be able to forgive her, if she is cheating. He loves her very much. Bernice sucked on a peppermint and turned on the radio to quiet her thoughts, as she waited patiently for her family to come out of the house.

When the children walked out the front door, Dana and Ashley walked to her car. The twins hopped into Jackie's car. Jackie walked up to her mother, explaining that Damon would follow in his car and leave once everybody was settled.

Bernice was fine with the plan, but she didn't understand why Damon was sticking around. Why was he with Jackie and not with his family?

The drive to the house was quiet. The girls were in the back asleep. Her mind wandered to the vehicle following her, and once again Bernice wanted to know why Damon and Jackie were together tonight.

Jada met them outside, as they all pulled up. Jackie and Jada were ten years apart, and they did not get along. Jada resented Jackie for her princess attitude, always wanting her way as a child and as an adult. She pouted, if she didn't get her way, and most of the time her mother would give in. It pleased Jada that their father would stand his ground and not always let Jackie have her way. He finally had enough, and left Bernice to raise their two daughters on her own. At least, that's what Jada thought happened.

"Why is Damon here," Jada asked? "I know you don't expect me to babysit, do you?" She spoke with a nasty tone, her hands positioned on her hips. She looked at her mother.

"Relax Jada," Bernice exclaimed! "I'm taking care of them, while Tony is in the hospital."

"Why didn't you come up to the hospital," Jackie asked. "Didn't you get my message?"

"I just got your message, because I ended up working some overtime," she said. "How is Tony doing anyway," her tone softened, as she thought of her nephew?

"He needs a blood transfusion," Bernice told her. "I'll fill you in, but first let's get these children in the house."

She peered at Damon with an evil look, as he made his way up the sidewalk. She didn't care much for Damon.

"What the heck are you looking at," Damon snapped at Jada?

"Hmm, that's what I'm trying to figure out," Jada clapped back.

Damon smacked his lips and headed back to the car.

"I know your lazy tail is going to help get these bags of your nieces and nephew in the house," Jada called after him, believing like the rest of Damon's family that he's lazy and doesn't have any direction for his life.

"Don't worry about me," Damon replied. "You do you."

"Ugh, you are such a sorry son of a gun, oooh," Jada vented, shaking her head in disgust.

"Will you two stop it," Jackie begged? "My son is in the hospital fighting for his life, and this is the last thing the children and I need right now!"

Tears began to run down Jackie's face. Damon and Jada were going to have to find a way to get along for the children's sake.

"Wait a minute," Jada continued suspiciously. "You have that big house with David. Why are you bringing them here?" Jada didn't like having children around. They were loud and messed with everything.

Jackie sighed, "none of your business, Jada." An argument was brewing, and she didn't have the strength to battle her sister. Jackie grabbed Ashley's hand, pushing past her sister to get in the house.

Jada put her arms around the twins, escorting them in the front door. Damon followed behind with their suitcases.

The children were already upstairs by the time Damon placed the bags at the bottom of the stairs. Jackie was sitting on the couch.

Bernice came and sat next to her daughter, as Damon was making his way to the couch. She politely thanked Damon, as if to tell him he was no longer needed.

"Mama, Damon is just helping," Jackie responded, not liking the accusatory tone in her mother's voice.

"It's ok Jackie...see you later," Damon said, walking out the door. He didn't understand why Bernice was speaking to him that way, but it didn't matter anymore.

In the present...

Jackie brought her mind back to the moment. For the past week, the traumatic memories surrounding her son's accident and its aftermath were haunting her. Fortunately, Tony was finally well enough to come home. She sat next to Damon, as he entered the hospital parking lot. Apprehension gripped her, because she wasn't sure how Tony would react, when David was not there to bring him home.

Inside the hospital, Tony sat on his hospital bed. He waited anxiously for his parents, so the hospital could discharge him. He missed his family and didn't understand why he hadn't seen his father or siblings, since he came out of the coma. The last time he was hospitalized, his dad stayed with him all day and all night. He asked his relatives, but he couldn't get an answer out of anyone. As he was thinking, his mother and Damon came into the room.

"Hi baby," Jackie said softly, walking over to kiss his forehead.

Tony was happy to see her, even though she's come to visit him daily. He was confused at the absence of his father. "Where's Dad," Tony asked, turning to his mother?

"Sweetheart, we have something to tell you, but let's wait until we get to the car," Jackie replied, hoping there wouldn't be any resistance to the news that Damon was his father. Dana and Ashley had yet to accept Damon as their father, and Jackie feared Tony may have a hard time adjusting also.

"Why can't you tell me now," Tony asked? Deep down, he feared something bad had happened to his father.

"Hey slugger, let's go to the car," Damon interjected, putting his hand on Tony's shoulder. "I promise it's not as bad as you think." Damon was trying to stop Tony from causing a scene.

He eyed Damon and Jackie for a moment. His dad may punish him for being defiant, so he stood up to leave. Transport came into the room with a wheelchair to escort him out of the building. Tony grabbed his bag, and sat down, allowing the hospital employee to roll him to the hospital entrance.

The doctor gave them the discharge papers, before they entered the room. Jackie and Damon followed behind him, glancing down at the clean, shiny floors. The couple noticed their son hadn't said a word to them, since he left the room. As they were leaving the hospital, Tony hopped out of the chair and walked quickly into the parking lot area.

Jackie called out to him, "Tony stop!"

He stopped in the middle of the drop-off circle and didn't bother to look at his parents.

"Slow down," Jackie commanded when she stood in front of her son. His eyes were focused straight ahead. Again, he did not look at his mother. Jackie lifted his chin, so that she could look him in his eyes. "Damon and I will tell you what you want to know, but you have to be patient."

Tony just nodded his head, but his eyes never focused on his mother.

Jackie looked at Damon to get him to speak with Tony. Damon just put his arms around Tony and continued to walk toward the car.

Once they were seated inside the vehicle, Tony sat in the back-middle seat with his arms folded, waiting for them to speak.

Damon started the car.

"I thought you were going to tell me what happened to my dad," Tony muttered, with a frown on his face.

Jackie looked at Damon again. He hadn't shifted into reverse yet. She nudged him to speak. Damon turned to look at Tony.

"Tony, this may be hard for you to hear, but I'm your father, not David," he said softly.

Tony stared at Damon, as if he were bluffing. He finally looked at his mother to gauge her expression. Jackie nodded her head to confirm what Damon said. Tony sat for a moment, processing the information. He turned to look at Damon. "Who gave you permission," Tony asked, as he realized that the father who raised him was not waiting for him at home? Reaching for the door handle, he jumped out of the car.

Both Jackie and Damon jumped out with him. Jackie caught him, before he could take off running. "Don't run," she implored him.

Tears were streaming down his eyes. "Is my dad dead," Tony wanted to know, thinking only death would keep David from him?

"David is not dead, but he's left the state with Junior and Nakita," Jackie explained. "You, Ashley, and Dana will live with me."

Tony was crying harder now. It was the same reaction the other children had. He kept shaking his head. "This isn't right," he yelled. "It's not fair!"

Jackie embraced her son. She didn't realize the magnitude of the devastation her children would suffer. Her emotions boiled over like a volcano, and tears stained her face. Tony hugged his mother in a show of comfort. She looked into his familiar hazelnut eyes, mirroring his father's concerned expression. Shame and regret moved fleetingly through her mind, as her son's love reminded her to embrace hope for a future with Damon.

Jackie urged her son to get back in the car. As the heat from the morning sun beat down on the hood of Damon's vehicle, he drove Jackie and Tony to Bernice's home. After helping Tony get settled, Damon left, nursing feelings of rejection once again.

In the coming months, Damon's world turned chaotic. Life couldn't have gotten any worse. He missed his brother something terrible and had never felt so alone. *How did it come to this?* He thought to himself. *Why didn't I leave her alone?* His father was right, he knew better than to mess around with another man's wife, especially his own brother's spouse. Now, the people he cared about the most avoided him like the plague. His mother may not say so, but deep down he believed that she blamed him for David moving to Atlanta with the twins.

The next move he needed to make would not be an easy one. Jackie was hounding him to come around more, pressuring him to commit to her and their relationship. He felt awful, but there was no way to continue as a couple. They were already ostracized by the family, and no one approved of it. Jackie left the man that cared so much for her to be with him, but he couldn't give her what his brother gave her. Both of their lives came crashing down at the same time.

There was no way to fix what they had already done. He wished he could make things right between Jackie and David. However, if he were in his brother's shoes, there was no way he would take a woman like that back. If they'd only been together once, maybe there would be a chance for reconciliation. He thought about the years that he and Jackie were intimate. Clearly, she never loved David, and he knew it. It wasn't like his brother wasn't warned. Numerous people tried to tell him. Damon even warned him, but David brushed it off like it was nothing.

Now, he had to tell Jackie that he's moving on, and she needs to do the same. The children are going to suffer from this. They were used to having both parents in the home. There was no way to tell how things will go from this point.

How can I be so stupid, he asked himself? All of this turmoil and dysfunction happened, because he was selfish. *I have to find a way to make this right.* He reached out to Aunt Gladys for advice, and her response was for him to pray and ask God for guidance. She also asked him to give David time to heal, and told him that it was time for him to step up to the plate and care for his children.

Damon didn't receive his aunt's advice well, because he didn't know God well enough to talk to him or trust him. Damon didn't know what to do. He didn't make a whole lot of money to begin with, let alone enough to care for his children with Jackie.

He needed to make a career change. Focusing on his regrets, Damon lamented his decision to not get a college degree. A side hustle would come in handy right now or just picking up a second job. Working two jobs would help with the bills, but he wouldn't have time for the children or Jackie.

Chapter 8

David was sitting at the computer in his aunt's home office. She and her husband were back from their road trip but only for a day. He had found a home in Lilburn, Georgia. The closing was set for this Friday.

He had several things to figure out for himself and his children. The new home needed furnishing. The twins wanted to go home for Thanksgiving. He wanted to get his real estate investing going again. They also needed to find a good church home. The place his aunt and her family attended was alright, but he was looking for more. Still, it was hard to focus on his future, because his mind kept returning to the situation he'd left in Michigan.

David spoke to his sister Micki who gave him an ear full of the dysfunction the children were experiencing with Damon as their father. Dana was acting out. Ashley didn't speak much to anyone but her siblings, and Tony called his mother out on her cheating. Both Damon and Jackie went crying to their parents for help. Fortunately, Jada kept Micki abreast of what's going on with Jackie.

His heart went out to all three children, because their lives will never be the same. Dana texts him every day to tell him that she misses him and the twins. It was hard to hear the challenges the children were experiencing. They didn't deserve it, but his brother didn't deserve to get off the hook. If he brought the children here, then Damon should take care of them. His disrespectful, irresponsible brother wanted all the pleasure of sleeping with his wife with none of the responsibility. According to his family, Damon was mostly absent from the children's lives.

It'd been two months since they left, and the twins wanted to visit Michigan. It was dreadful just thinking that he would have to see Jackie, when he dropped the twins off in a few weeks. His aunt has been encouraging him to let go of what those two did, so that he could move on. David was ready to move forward with his life, but it wasn't easy to forgive Jackie or his brother.

David picked up his Bible. In Matthew 6:14, God reminded him of His word to forgive man their sins against you, so that He can forgive your sins. It was only through prayer that David was able to survive the emotional test. Reading God's Word helped David to release some judgmental thoughts about his brother and his wife.

Deep in thought, he didn't notice his Aunt Gladys was standing at the threshold smiling. David chuckled, when he saw his aunt gazing happily at him.

"You must have good news," he said to her. "I haven't seen you smile this broadly in a long time."

Gladys made her way into the office and took a seat in the small computer chair. "It brings me joy, when I can be of help to you children," she explained. "I'd understand if you don't want us to do it, but we'd be glad to take the twins to visit Michigan for you." She sat calmly waiting for an answer.

David waited for her to finish, but she offered nothing else. He realized she was done talking, but he had no idea they'd planned a trip. "Are you going to Michigan," he asked?

"Your uncle and I discussed it, and we've decided to take a trip back to Michigan for Thanksgiving," she explained. "We could take the twins to Jackie, if you'd like." She clapped her hands together in anticipation of his answer.

David was a little confused. His aunt vowed that she'd never step foot in Michigan again, after they were harassed by Bloomfield Hills police while attending Derrick's funeral three years ago. "I thought you didn't want to go back to Michigan again," he said.

Gladys shrugged her shoulders, as she spoke, "well I miss my sister, and I'm not afraid of the police any longer. Besides, that's where I grew up."

A smile crept onto his face, as he thought about the offer. "Of course, you may," David agreed. "I don't mind. I don't mind at all."

He stood up to hug his aunt, and she jumped out of her chair to meet him.

"You're a little excited," he teased her, as they embraced.

Gladys was ecstatic. Her husband wouldn't go, unless they could take the twins with them. She knew she wouldn't want to stay home, after they returned from the Poconos, a trip they were leaving for the next day. When they pulled apart, she hurriedly went to tell her husband the good news.

David was still grinning from ear to ear. He caught a break, because he didn't have to meet up with his estranged wife.

A sense of relief came over him, and David decided to go furniture shopping before picking up the twins from school. The closing was in the middle of the week, but they wouldn't move until the house was furnished. Using Google maps, he traveled through the streets of Riverdale to the tree-lined suburban roads near Lilburn. He picked stores near his new home, stopping on Pleasant Hill Road to choose appliances. It occurred to him that he probably should have had someone to accompany him. At the same time, shopping alone helped take his mind off his family's problems.

David's new home housed seven bedrooms, but you couldn't tell looking from the outside in the front yard. When you walk into the front door, the dining room was to the right. Mahogany floors gave the home an air of elegance throughout. Each bathroom, including the master bath was professionally painted with colorful accent walls. A little further in the home on the left was the master bedroom. A massive kitchen was accessible near the living room. Behind the dining room stood a hallway where the laundry room was located, leading to the garage. An elegant staircase stood in between the living and dining rooms.

Even though the new home was beautiful, David prayed that his family filled it with love. He couldn't help but remember that their home in Michigan was also beautiful throughout. *As for me and my house, we will serve the Lord,* David said quietly to himself, as he continued his shopping to furnish the majestic home.

Its upstairs housed another living room and two bedrooms on each end of the living room. A full bathroom was just at the top of the stairs on the left. The basement included another living area with four bedrooms and a full bathroom. The home was big enough to accommodate all of his family, if they chose to come for Christmas.

He'd decided to shop for the appliances first, because David didn't like the outdated stove and refrigerator already in the home. A tall, stainless-steel refrigerator caught his eye. David motioned for a sales rep to give him the item's tag, so he could purchase it. Next, he chose an electric stove with French doors and a warming station.

David checked his watch, as he moved through the aisles. He remembered that the laundry room isn't in the basement, so it wouldn't be a hassle to carry clothes up and down the stairs. Choosing a red, high-efficiency washer and dryer set, David moved to the register.

David was happy with the high-quality appliances he selected. Shopping made him feel good and furniture was next on his list. Everything was coming together. He grew up in an area with little crime and wanted the same for the twins. With the new home in a good area, his children are transferring to Gwinnett County Schools, one of the best and largest school systems in Georgia.

The furniture store was down the street on the same road. As he walked into the store, a five-piece, dark blue upholstery sectional caught his attention. It had three reclining seats, two cup holders, and a hidden storage console. Thankfully, the item was available and on sale, because he also needed to buy three-bedroom sets.

He left Michigan so quickly that he'd left all the furniture behind. Purchasing new furniture was best for all three of them. The old furniture would only remind them of Jackie and the children in

Michigan. By the grace of God, he had an emergency fund and money in a mutual fund to get them started again.

Choosing the bedroom sets was the hardest. The twins were old enough to pick their own sets, but time was ticking. He wanted everything delivered by Saturday. That's the day the three of them were vacating his aunt and uncle's home. He decided that they would hang up their clothes, while they wait for the deliveries. The televisions and computers have already been purchased and are sitting in Aunt Gladys' storage room for safe keeping.

He purchased the best furniture possible, which meant that the three of them would enjoy seven-piece bedroom sets. With built in shelving and matching dressers, the furniture was sure to please the twins. After choosing a dark cherry, queen-sized set for himself, David's shopping adventure came to an end. He had a long drive back to Riverdale. Despite the weariness from shopping, David could hardly contain his excitement about the opportunity for a fresh start with his children. He knew the tangible items wouldn't replace their mother, but he hoped to also fill the home with lots of love.

Chapter 9

There was a knock at the bedroom door. Jackie got up to answer it. Her dad stood on the other side. Her heart skipped a beat. She wasn't expecting him to show up. "Dad, it's good to see you. Mom isn't here."

"I'm here to see you, sweetheart," Charles replied. "Your mother told me you and the children were here."

She stepped back, so he could come in. She had a big smile on her face. Jackie hugged her father, after she closed the door. "It's been a long-time since we've had alone time Dad. What have you been doing?"

"I'm just trying to live. Your mother tells me that you and David are getting a divorce." He took a seat on the bed.

"Wow Dad, straight to the point huh," Jackie sighed? "Yes, we are getting a divorce. I don't know why I stayed married to him for so long, but my heart has always been with Damon."

"Well, if that was the case, why did you marry him at all?" Her father had a judgmental tone and look on his face. Charles Sr. was known to attack those who have done wrong in their life.

Jackie looked down, "I don't know. I did love him once."

Charles shook his head. "You're just like your mother." He turned his head and looked around the bedroom.

"Dad, what are you doing here?" Jada came into the room.

They embraced and chatted for a bit. Jackie was still reeling about what her father had just stated.

"Dad, what do you mean I'm just like mama," she asked, shaking her head in bewilderment.

Charles sat back down on the bed and invited Jada to stick around. "I take it your mother has never told you the truth." He looked at his daughter. "Jackie honey, you did the exact same thing your mother did."

"What," Jackie and Jada exclaimed in unison!

Her father grabbed her hand. "Talk to your mother, find out how life has turned out for her since everything came into the light," he said, patting her hand and smiling at her. Charles called for his grandchildren. He decided to take them with him to give Jackie a chance to speak with her mother without interruption. "I'll keep them overnight, so you and your mother can have a heart to heart."

Jackie and Jada sat on the bed upset and mystified. Neither one of them knew what their father was talking about.

"Is Dad saying that mom had an affair, and that's why they broke up," Jada asked? She had a frown on her face, staring straight ahead at the wall.

Jackie was sobbing.

"Don't let him upset you. I don't know why Dad always talks in rid…"

Jackie pulled away from Jada, she shook her head. "He's not talking in riddles, Jada. Now I know why the boys don't talk to mom any more. Mom and dad didn't break up, because they couldn't get along. They broke up, because mom had an affair."

"How do you know this?"

"I overheard dad and Charles Jr. talking about it one day when we were over grandma and grandpa Eldridge's house. I was taking a nap in one of the spare bedrooms. I heard everything about mom and this man. I thought it was a dream, because you came and woke me up. I must have dozed off while listening to them. I can't believe this. That's why mama is so adamant about me going back to David.

She's alone and does not want the same for me. Only I won't be alone, because Damon is not going to leave me."

"Damon might not leave you, but you might leave him. Jackie, he's a leach. You said it yourself; he's always depending on you and David to take care of him. Can't you see that? If he can't take care of himself, then how is he going to take care of you or those children? Think about it," Jada cautioned.

"But that's nothing compared to what we've just learned," she continued. "You did the exact same thing mom did; she lied about her affair and so did you."

Dana came into the room. She stood in a slouch position. Jackie could see the events of the day were weighing heavy on her second oldest daughter. "Do we have to go with grandpa," she asked in a whiny voice.

"I think it would be best," Jackie replied. "Your dad and I as well as your grandmother have a lot to discuss and under the circumstances, Grandpa Charles is your best bet." Jackie could see that Dana was upset, but she knew Charles Sr. would see that they had a good time, doing something to take their mind off of things.

Dana sighed, "fine," as she turned and walked out the door. Dana didn't bother to close it back. She was disgusted and disappointed in her mother. Maybe leaving the home was a good idea and Grandpa Charles may have some answers to her questions.

As Bernice was pulling into her driveway, Charles was leaving with the grandchildren. She walked through the door and called out to her daughters. Both of them came running down the stairs to talk with her, "why didn't you tell us? Why did you lie about the affair?" Tears formed in Jackie's eyes again.

Her daughters surprised Bernice with the questions. She composed herself and began explaining, "I didn't know how to tell you, because I didn't want you to do the same thing to me that your brothers did. They disowned me, after they found out. Your brothers caught us together. You and Jada had gone out with my father, and the boys..."

She stopped, shaken and dejected. Her daughters had the same look that her sons had given her. There was no turning back; she may experience the same fate with her daughters. Bernice sat down on the couch. She wept uncontrollably, as Jackie embraced her in a big hug.

Jada sat staring at the floor. She couldn't believe that it was her mother who caused the family to break apart. All these years she believed it was because they didn't see eye to eye on raising Jackie. That's what she was told by her mother and grandmother, but that was a lie. Her mother committed adultery and kept the truth hidden until now. Jada went upstairs to her room and wept.

After Bernice got control of herself, Jackie began to question her about the affair. "So, who was this man mama?" Jackie was perplexed.

"He was your father's best friend, Harry Lyons." Bernice couldn't look Jackie in the eye. She and her sister know Harry all too well.

Jackie was floored. Her mouth gaped open, as she removed her arm from off her mother's shoulders.

Harry Lyons was Charles' best friend; he was also married. The Lyons had five children who grew up with Jackie and her siblings. She knew that Harry divorced his wife but didn't know the details. One day the Lyons' were around, and the next day they were gone. No one ever said why they stopped coming around, and she didn't bother to ask.

Jackie stood up and started pacing. "Oh my God, this is starting to make sense. Now I know why Amber stopped talking to me. We were so close, born two days apart, and shared a lot of secrets. It was a mutual friend of ours that told me that the Lyons moved to

California, but I had no idea why." She stopped to look at her mother.

Bernice kept looking down. Guilt and shame overwhelmed her. She never wanted her daughters to know the truth. It was by the grace of God that neither her brothers, nor father ever spoke on it.

"Mama, what happened with you and Harry?"

"He turned out to be the biggest jerk ever," Bernice explained. "All the while we were together, I thought he was a go-getter, a provider, and a man of means. It turns out that he was addicted to gambling. He ran through the family savings, put the house up for collateral, and borrowed from friends and family to support his habit. Joanne left him because of his gambling, she found out about the affair from your father. They were already in California when Charles told her about it."

"You didn't answer my question," Jackie insisted. "I want to know why you two didn't stay together."

"Jackie, I just told you he was addicted to gambling. We didn't come together, because he blew through everything he had. Then he started taking money and borrowing money from me to gamble it away. He really believed that he would hit it big one day, and that we'd be set for life. That day never came. He lost everything, and his family disowned him.

One day he came to the house while you and your sister were gone. We spent the day together; the house phone rang; I got up to answer it. Your grandmother was on the other end. When I hung up the phone from her, Harry was gone and so was the money in my purse. I don't know how he found it, but he found my purse that I'd hidden in the front closet. That man was so desperate, he didn't even put my purse back, just left it sitting on the couch. That was the last time I saw him. I heard through the grapevine that he was strung out on drugs."

Bernice finally looked at her daughter.

Jackie thought about what her mother told her. She chose the next set of words carefully. "And you think the same thing is going to happen to me," she asked? "You think Damon is going to just walk out my life, leaving me to raise three children by myself."

"Yes, that's exactly what I believe. When have you ever known that man to be responsible? No one knows where he lives or..."

Jackie interrupted her mother. "I'm sorry mama that the man you left dad for left you, but that's not going to happen to me. Damon and I love each other, and we're going to raise our children together. I'll appreciate if you stay out of my business with my family, seeing as you broke our family up." Jackie started to walk upstairs.

"Don't you see that you're headed in the same direction," Bernice cautioned.

Jackie ignored her mother's comments, and continued to walk upstairs into her bedroom.

Days had gone by since her conversation with her mother. The relationship with her mother was strained, and Bernice wasn't open to talking with Jackie about her problems. All her mother would say is make it work with David, before it's too late. She didn't want to be with David, because she loved Damon. Jackie was overwhelmed with the entire situation, so she went to visit her dad for advice and support.

Her father met her at the door. "Hello sweetheart," he said. There was a big smile on his face. He reached out and embraced his daughter.

"Hi Dad," Jackie replied.

"So, to what do I owe the pleasure of this visit," he asked? After sitting down in his favorite comfortable, leather recliner, he motioned for Jackie to sit on the couch.

Jackie let out a long, deep sigh. "My life is in shambles," she muttered. "I haven't found a place decent enough for me and the children to live, and mom is counting down the days to the deadline that she gave us to move. The count is visible right on the calendar in the kitchen."

Charles Sr. nodded his head to let her know that he understood. He chose his words carefully. "Have you spoken to your mother about letting you stay longer," he inquired?

Jackie looked down. "I've tried to tell her that I need more time, but she's not listening," Jackie replied, shrugging her shoulders.

"Did you check into the homes that Jada told you about," he wondered?

"Yes, and they're not suitable," Jackie responded.

She knew what was coming next. Her sister and cousins have all said the same. *'You want your cake and eat it too.'* She just wanted a decent place to raise her children.

Charles took a deep breath. "Sweetheart, I'm afraid you have some hard choices to make," he reasoned.

Jackie leaned her head to the side in the direction of her father with a confused look on her face. "What do you mean," she asked?

Charles sat up straighter in his chair. "You're looking to have the same lifestyle that you had with David in your relationship with Damon," Charles replied. "Unfortunately, Damon's not yet living up to his fullest potential."

Jackie wanted to interject, but her father stopped her.

"Sweetheart, your current income alone is not enough for you to enjoy the material things that you and your children had when David was around," her father explained. "Three possible options for you include the judge awarding you a lot of money, Damon changing his career, or you earnestly seeking the kingdom of God."

81

Jackie thought about what her father said about the judge for a moment. "Do you think he will give me a big award?"

Charles shrugged his shoulders. "It depends on what type of lawyer David hires," Charles replied, noting that his daughter ignored his reference to God. "I know him to be a well-managed financial man, so I'm sure he's going to get the best attorney money can buy."

Tears began to form in her eyes. "What if he doesn't award me anything," she asked, putting her hands over her eyes in despair?

Charles came over to his daughter and wrapped her in his arms. It hurt his heart to see his daughter crying.

When she gained her composure, she had another question to ask her father. She'd been wanting to know for some time but hadn't found the time to ask until now. "Dad, why didn't you mention to us what mom did to you?" She looked up at him.

Charles could see the hurt in her eyes, because he'd never sat down and discussed with his daughters his real reason for leaving Bernice.

He thought about the events, which took place leading up to his discovery that Bernice was cheating on him and his decision to subsequently leave. He pulled away from Jackie, so he could look her in her eyes. "Your mother wanted to be the one to tell you, and she led me to believe that you all knew," he replied. "I would have told you whatever you wanted to know."

"Our brothers never mentioned it either," she uttered.

Charles laughed inwardly. "They were reluctant to tell you, because at first I didn't even believe them when they told me."

He remembered it like yesterday. Charles began to explain to Jackie that the boys saw their mother and his best friend, Harry, together. They came to him in confidence. He didn't believe them and punished the boys for telling lies on their mother.

Charles Jr. and Eric hired a neighborhood investigator to get proof. It was only with photographic evidence was Charles able to come to grips with the reality of his wife's betrayal. Much like David, he loved Bernice completely, and only irrefutable proof would have caused him to leave his marriage.

"Your brothers didn't want to hurt you," Charles continued.

Jackie looked at her father intently. "Do you think I am doing the same thing that mom did?"

Charles wasn't prepared to reveal what he really thought of Jackie and Damon together. "Do you really want my opinion," he asked her softly?

Jackie looked out the window and nodded.

"I think you're making a horrible mistake.," Charles replied bluntly.

"I love him, and he loves me," she cried. It seems like no one cares about her happiness. She was miserable with David and was tired of living a lie.

"That may be sweetheart, but you married his brother and stayed married to him for fifteen years," her father counseled her. "Why did you wait till after you gave birth to five babies to reveal to any of us that it was Damon you loved all this time?"

"I didn't know how to tell him," she responded. "I loved David, but not like I love Damon." Jackie stopped talking and slouched down in her seat. It was no use explaining herself to anyone. Only she and Damon knew what they were going through. Deep down inside, she felt defeated. "I should have told him a long time ago," she agreed with her father.

Her dad nodded his head. "You'll pull through this, sweetheart," he said. "I do think that you should reevaluate your definition of love, though."

Jackie looked at her father, noting the disappointment in his eyes. "Love is not just the warm feeling in the pit of your stomach or a kiss that makes your toes curl," he explained. "Love is action."

"What do you mean," Jackie asked?

"I mean that kindness, unselfishness, and devoted service are loving actions," he replied. "The way you and David took care of each other and the children is love in action."

"Love in action," Jackie repeated her father.

"Every time that you give of yourself to family by sharing, cooking, or forgiving, you are showing love," he continued. "When you remember what makes another happy, that's love."

"I love Damon," she insisted.

"Hmmm, I submit to you that you have not had an opportunity to love Damon in the real sense," her father replied. "Love in a marital relationship can only be shown over years of commitment.

Jackie looked her father deep in his eyes and wondered if he loved her mother. "Do you love mom," she asked?

Charles smiled softly. "I can tell you that I agree with your mother," he said. "I believe that you love David more than you realize."

"Why don't you bring the children here this weekend, so you can have some time with your mother to work things out?"

Jackie was pleased to hear her dad offer some help. Both she and Damon had a lot of family in the tri-county area, but no one was offering any assistance. She gave her dad a big hug, as she left for work. She was so thankful to have him in her life. Three words continually passed through her mind that evening, *Love in action.*

Jackie's talk with her father last month had helped her to reorganize her priorities. She'd never thought of all the mundane things that she did daily as love in action. Somehow, the slight shift in her perception helped her to enjoy her life a little more.

The children were busy packing their belongings. It was the day before Labor Day. School would start on Tuesday. Bernice had made plans to dine with friends. Jada was getting ready to spend the day with her boyfriend. Damon's family was gathering at his parents' home, but she wasn't welcome. Damon and the children were invited. Her father and brothers extended an invitation to dine with them and some other family members, but she declined and decided to spend the day alone. Damon tried to talk her into going to her father's home, but she wouldn't hear of it and felt her brothers and other family would just lecture her about how wrong she was.

The children were all gathering their clothes, electronics and personal items. Jackie and Damon came in to bring more boxes.

Tony looked up at his mother and father. He sighed loudly. "I don't see why we just can't stay here with grandma," he complained, folding his arms across his chest.

"We can't stay here, sweetheart," Jackie huffed.

"Why can't we," he asked?

"Because grandma doesn't want us here," Ashley piped in.

"That's not true," Tony exclaimed!

"It is true," Dana insisted, walking over to her brother. "Grandma is selling the house and moving into something smaller. Mom and Uncle Damon don't make enough to care for this house."

"Don't you mean, daddy," Ashley retorted sarcastically?

Tony and Dana roared in laughter.

"What's so funny," Damon interjected, not liking the joke at his expense? Damon looked each child in their eyes. Anger swelled up in him because they refused to acknowledge him as their father.

"You're our uncle, and we shall address you as such," Dana spoke for the three of them.

"Dana, you will not disrespect your father," Jackie exclaimed!

Dana yelled back at her mother. "He's not my father, and I wish you all would quit saying he is," she proclaimed!

"Now you look here, young lady," Damon raised his voice. "I will not have you talking to your mother that way."

Dana started to walk out of the room, but Damon blocked her.

"Do you hear me," he insisted?

"I don't have to take orders from you," Dana replied defiantly. She stood there with her hands on her hips, eyeing Damon fiercely.

"Damon," Bernice called, as she climbed the stairs to stop the ruckus.

Damon turned to Bernice, giving a disapproving look for her interference.

Jada came out of her room. "Dana, why don't you go and call your dad," she said, offering Dana her cell phone?

Dana took the phone and turned to look at Damon with a triumphant expression on her face before heading downstairs.

"Bernice, you shouldn't...," Damon said.

Bernice stopped him from speaking with a wave of her hand. "You two are going to have to give them some time to process all of this," she muttered.

Jackie came to Damon's defense. "I will not have her being disrespectful to me or to anyone for that matter," Jackie retorted.

"I'm not saying you have to let her disrespect you, but you can't expect her to immediately jump on board with Damon being their father," Bernice explained.

Jackie thought about that for a moment. Maybe her mother was right. It wasn't fair to ask the children to begin calling Damon their father right away. Especially since, David has been a father to the children for all their lives. Jackie looked at Damon and then her mother. "You're right; I need to... we need to give them time to adjust."

Damon couldn't believe what he was hearing. Jackie was turning against him and siding with her mother. He stood there with his arms folded and stared at Jackie with disappointment. "I can't believe you just said that Jackie," he uttered.

Jackie and her mother looked at each other in silent agreement. Damon was going to have to learn to be patient, and give them all time to accept the change.

"Damon, we have to think of the children," she replied. "David has been with them since before birth." Jackie looked at Damon, hoping he'd understand.

"I've been there for them just as much as David," Damon retorted in frustration. He turned on his heels and headed down the stairs. On the way out the door, Damon heard Dana talking on the phone with Junior.

While Junior spoke to Dana, he told her about their plan. They were encouraging the family to come together for the Christmas holiday. Junior and Nakita missed their family something awful. Unfortunately, their father wasn't sure, if they would make it back to Michigan anytime soon. Their mother was struggling financially. They decided that if they didn't go home for Christmas, then the family, including Damon and their mother, should come to Georgia.

Dana and Junior discussed everything that had taken place since the family separated. It seemed like none of the relatives wanted Damon or Jackie around. Most were even against taking in the children to help Jackie and Damon out. Dana overheard that Deloris and Joseph wanted Damon to take care of his responsibilities.

The twins expressed their disappointment at their parents' separation. They loved Georgia, though. It was hot but fun. Nakita and Junior told Dana about their new friends but assured her that they still missed all three of them. Aunt Gladys also kept them active by taking them around town to introduce them to southern living. Still, it wasn't the same as living together as a family.

Dana voiced her frustration with her parents arguing all the time. Plus, she hated the thought of calling Damon her father. Aunt Micki told her it would become easier, but right now Dana just wanted to see David.

The twins started to feel bad. Their close-knit family seemed to be falling apart. According to Dana, Damon wasn't around much either.

After they hung up the phone, the twins rethought their plans to have everyone visit. Confrontation was not their forte', and they tried to avoid it at all costs. Their parents didn't argue in front of them, and they were surprised that Dana said she'd heard Jackie and Damon arguing.

Nakita and Junior decided to bring up the subject of Christmas with their grandparents. Picking up the phone again, Junior called Grandma Bernice. Nakita took her cellular phone out of her pocket to dial Grandma Deloris. They had a few months to convince them to make the trip.

Dana came upstairs to give Jada the phone, before she went outside to sit on the front porch with Tony and Ashley. Jackie sat in her room looking around. There were a lot of memories in this place. She hated that she had to let it go. There were several desperate attempts to convince her mother to let her keep the house. Ultimately, Bernice decided to sell the house to Micki, David and Damon's sister. Micki had gotten into real estate investing, snapping up deals and quickly flipping them to make a profit.

Jackie reluctantly asked Micki to allow her to live in the house with her children. She thought Micki would have a little compassion for her nieces and nephew. Jackie would have to move them from Oakland County to a totally different school district, but Micki didn't care.

The conversation they had about the house didn't go well. Her sister-in-law gloated over her misfortunes and taunted her for sleeping with Damon. After the discussion, Jackie was convinced that it was useless to try to mend the broken relationship with the Campbell family.

She thought back to better times when she and David were together. Unfortunately, those days were long gone. For the first time, Jackie realized that she missed some aspects of her former life. Now, her mother-in-law gave her the cold shoulder. Joseph tried to reason with his wife, but she wouldn't hear of it. Deloris refused to look at Jackie and pretty much ignored her whenever they were around one another.

She was supposed to be happy once she got with Damon, but they were both miserable. Damon's family practically shunned them. He wasn't welcome to anyone's home anymore. In the past, Damon spent most of his time at the home she and David shared or at his parents' home.

Her family treated her differently also. She could barely reach her cousins and brothers. Her cousin had a birthday party last month, and Jackie knew the family was whispering about her behind her back. Some of her relatives were surprised that she and Damon showed up. They did not feel welcomed.

Jada informed her that everyone was disgusted, disappointed, and embarrassed that she would sleep with her husband's brother. Their cousin hadn't extended an invitation to her. Jada said she told her about the party, but didn't think Jackie would show up.

She was beginning to think that maybe her mother and father were right about her decision to be with Damon. He wouldn't be able to provide for her or the children the way David did. The children were used to a life of traveling, eating out at restaurants, extracurricular activities, the best health care, and designer clothes. They enjoyed a rather good life, before she left David.

Ever since she and David split, they hadn't eaten out at a restaurant, unless their Grandpa Charles treated them. Dana would have to give up cheerleading. Tony couldn't bowl anymore. Ashley will have to lay dancing aside. She and Damon couldn't even afford to take the children to a fast-food restaurant.

Fortunately, sometimes David sent some money to help with clothes and food, and it was a great help. She never realized how much it cost to support her family. When she was married, David would hand her the check book. and she would purchase whatever they needed. She never paid attention to what she spent, because they always had more than enough money.

As a stay-at-home mom, the children kept her busy, especially during the summer. When Dana entered pre-school years ago, it gave her more time to spend with Damon. She reflected on the times they shared together. Those were good times, but it wasn't like that now.

Life's pressures altered the dynamics of her relationship with Damon. They seem to disagree about everything, including how to rear the children, living arrangements, and grocery shopping. Damon was used to going without food and expected the children to do the same.

Jackie would starve, before she let her children go hungry. It was finally clear to her why her mother warned her about getting close to Damon. She decided that she was going to stop lamenting her past mistakes. She had to plan for her future.

Her present challenge included finding a stable home for the children. Christmas was quickly approaching, and she barely had any money for her family. She missed Junior and Nakita, but she realized that they were better off with David. With a sigh, she sent Damon a text message to remind him to come visit them after work.

Damon heard the buzzing from his phone in his pocket. He noticed that a text message came through, but didn't read it right away. He was busy heat-treating car parts at his factory job. It was monotonous, boring work and could be dangerous, if he wasn't careful. All day, he'd put the parts in the oven for several seconds and remove them, dropping each part in a bin. After so many parts had been treated, someone would come along and empty the bin to package the parts.

He thought about his life and started scolding himself for not pursuing a career. His brothers and sister earned college degrees and worked in professional positions. His parents tried desperately to get him to finish his college education, but he wasn't interested. For years, he worked odd jobs. He had enough to pay his bills, and that made him happy.

Unfortunately, paying bills for one person was very different than paying bills for a family of five. His job didn't pay much, and he had a lot of mouths to feed. Jackie and the children were depending on him. He just wanted to cut out and run from it all.

At those times, he thought about his children. Damon always loved them, even when he was just an uncle. A part of him doesn't think that he and Jackie are going to make it, but he'd always take care of the children.

Chapter 10

The twins were excited to go home for Thanksgiving, but a twist of events shattered their dreams. The motorhome broke down while his aunt and uncle were coming back from the Poconos. David hated to disappoint the twins, but they had to stay in Georgia this time. Fortunately, the twins were excited to hear that the family was coming to visit for Christmas. Only Dana from their mother's household was coming to Georgia during the holidays. He didn't tell his children that she wouldn't receive any gifts because of her behavior. He wasn't even sure, if Dana knew.

David's cousin Mitchell hosted Thanksgiving for the family in Atlanta this year. The twins were invited to stay the weekend, since they were going to be in attendance. Mitchell agreed to drop them off on Sunday after church service, and the twins were excited.

On Thanksgiving evening, Micki called to give David the scoop on the family's holiday celebration. Chris' wife Trina prepared all the food herself, with a little help from her two older daughters. Everyone came to the dinner except Jackie. Damon showed up with his three children. During dinner, his phone kept ringing or vibrating, because Jackie kept calling him. She wanted to be with the family, but felt like no one wanted her around. The children were glad to be away from her, because she complained and fussed at them constantly. Micki kept going on and on about everything and everyone, until suddenly David had enough. He politely ended the call for his peace of mind.

He walked across the room to a stack of books that he'd picked up from the library. Learning a new language would keep his mind focused on something productive. Picking up the French book, David began to repeat the simplest words. "Oui," he said to himself with a smile.

David spent the first part of Thanksgiving recess going over French and Turkish words he'd learned. The sound of gospel music flowed through the main living room where he sat studying the words and phrases. Other than the music, the house was still and quiet without the twins blasting the television set. The stillness gave him time to concentrate, but also left him with a feeling of solitude, which he wasn't used to experiencing.

David found his mind drifting to the dating website, where he'd met a young lady who was also learning Turkish. He checked his watch. They'd set up a first date, and he had to meet her shortly. Leaving the living room, he walked briskly to hop in the shower

April left the office to meet an intriguing man she'd met online. She drove away from the city heading north on I-75/85. The sermon from Sunday's service resonated in her spirit, as she thought about all the obstacles she'd experienced in her life. She dreamed of beginning a new chapter and hoped the man she was meeting would help in that regard.

'Trials come to make you stronger,' she recalled her pastor's words from Sunday service. 'God will never leave you nor forsake you, and he'll bring you through it.'

She put down the visor to block the early afternoon sunlight, as traffic on the interstate grew during the lunchtime rush. Her stomach started gurgling from hunger, as she steered the car onto one of the Marietta exits toward a small diner. As April walked in, she noted two people were sitting at booths in front of the window. The bar was directly in front of her, and it curved around to the other side of the diner. Behind the bar, diners sat at four tables in the middle of the floor, and behind them the small booths were packed.

April took a seat at the bar, positioning herself on the bar stools, which were red with stainless steel casings. The stool she chose was padded well. There was only one seat remaining at the bar; it placed her between two gentlemen. The man on her left seemed to be accompanied by a lady, and the one to her right appeared to be alone. He was focusing on his tablet, and she wasn't sure if it was the same man that she'd met online.

"What can I get for you," asked the waitress, with a southern drawl? The young, black female, sported a bob-like, old-school hairstyle.

"I'll have a cup of tea, while I decide," April replied, as she picked up the menu.

David was busy looking at posts from the different social media platforms. Some of the content was worth viewing, while others he ignored completely. It was just a way to pass time, until he met his date for the afternoon. He had noticed the beautiful woman on a Christian dating site a week ago, and found her profile interesting. He was especially drawn to the fact that she spoke fluent Turkish, a language he chose to learn to keep his mind occupied after moving to Atlanta. From the corner of his eye, David saw the young lady sitting next to him, and he realized it was his date. Her picture did not do her justice. Deep down inside, he wasn't sure that he was ready for a new relationship. Yet, David felt drawn to this woman online and now in person. He found himself staring at her in awe.

"Hi," April said. "Are you David?"

"Yes," David replied. "Nice to meet you in person, April."

April raised her eyebrows. '*Good heavens,*' she thought silently. "*He is gorgeous.*'

"My pleasure," April replied, "It's great to finally meet someone that shares so many common interests."

A knowing look crept upon his face. "I feel you on that one," he replied.

A thought came across her mind. "Do you speak Turkish well?"

"Evet." (Yes). He smiled at her, as he responded in Turkish. She seemed pleased, and the two continued to speak in English and Turkish, as they enjoyed eating lunch with one another.

Later, as David drove home, he thought about his encounter with April. It was the most fun he had with a female in over a decade.

Not once did he think of Jackie, and he believed that this new friendship was just what he needed.

His mind raced, as he tried to remember all the things that she'd shared with him. He didn't know where she lived or worked. He wanted to find out more about April, and he couldn't wait to see her again.

A few weeks later, David decided to shop for the twins and the family, since they were coming to Georgia for Christmas. He missed everyone, except Jackie and Damon.

David wanted Dana to visit, because she begged him almost every day to live with him. She refused to accept Damon as her father and according to Bernice, Damon was not happy about her attitude. Tony and Ashley were coming to grips with David as an uncle and welcomed Damon as their father slowly.

David walked around the mall. The twins wanted updated iPads and iPhones. He could have easily gone to an electronics store down the road, but he wanted to walk around inside a mall. He remembered an Apple store at the mall and decided to buy the gifts there.

Entering the food court, he noticed the eating area was packed. People filled most of the seats near the restaurants, as diners rested and ate during the holiday shopping trips. He found a vacant seat at a table with two guys, so David decided to rest a bit. There were so many food choices, and he couldn't decide on what to eat.

Choosing Chinese, David placed his jacket on the chair to hold the seat, returning minutes later with Mongolian beef and fried rice. Suddenly, he noticed a familiar face in the crowd, and she was walking toward him with a big smile on her face. It was April from the dating site. Conflicting schedules didn't allow them to reconnect after their first date. He thought they may never meet again.

Standing up to greet her, David noticed that April Lockhart was stunning with a slender physique and flawless brown skin. Her long, thick, and dark brown hair framed her face, accentuating her angelic, light brown eyes.

"Hey David, it's good to see you," April said, her smile captivating him, just as it did the first time they met.

"It's good to see you as well," David responded, offering her a seat across from him. His smile expanded across his face, and he hoped he didn't look like a giddy idiot.

"So, what brings you to the mall by yourself," he asked?

"I was going to ask you the same thing," she grinned at him, noting his athletic physique. He was a handsome man, and she figured he was married or dating someone. Still, she glanced at his hand and noted that he wore no wedding band. "I'm just doing some last-minute shopping, before my family goes out of town," she replied.

She has a family? David assumed that she was married. *Why in the world was she on a dating site then?* "You're not traveling with your husband and children," he asked? It was unbelievable for him to think that a man would leave his beautiful wife during the holiday season.

"No," April looked down at the table and giggled. "It's my parents and sisters who are going away for the holidays. They are visiting a family member, but I've decided to stay behind."

"Oh, I'm sorry, I thought you were talking about…never mind," David cut his thought short.

"Ok, your turn," she teased, smiling and waiting for an explanation.

David was perplexed. "I'm sorry?" He didn't know what she meant.

"Why are you here by yourself?"

"Oh! Well, my parents and siblings are coming here from Michigan for Christmas, and I'm shopping for my twins, parents, nieces and nephew."

April gasped after he mentioned the twins. "You have twins?" Her smile broadened.

"Yes, but it's a little more complicated," he said. "I'll tell you about it someday."

"Ok, is their mother in the picture?" April didn't want to come in between a family. She had her share of infidelity from her own marriage.

"Not any more, we're divorcing after a decade and a half, and she lives in Michigan with the rest of her children."

"Wow, fifteen years, I'm so sorry." April was stunned that a man so gorgeous was divorcing. It's none of her business but she had to ask. "What happened, if you don't mind me asking."

David explained to her everything from start to finish. He had no intention of revealing his life story to her so soon. Somehow, it didn't feel right to keep it from her.

"Wow," April responded! That was all she could say at first. "I'm sorry you had to go through that experience. Your story is very much like my story." She wanted to tell David what she had been through but an alarm on her phone sounded reminding her that she needed to leave.

The two exchanged phone numbers and agreed to continue the conversation later that night.

April couldn't stop smiling after her encounter with David. She couldn't figure out why she was so jubilant. It never occurred to her that she would see him again, now that she has, her mind kept reeling about their talks. Her mind drifted back to her marriage with Robbie. Like David, her husband left her for her best friend.

April and Robbie were married at their parents' bidding. Arranged marriages weren't popular in the US. Nevertheless, since the business both families operated would one day belong to both of them, the parents encouraged Robbie and April to marry. They'd grown up together and knew each other well. Neither of them had any romantic entanglements, so they agreed. It wasn't an easy decision to make, but they trusted their parents' judgment.

William and Angela White had four daughters. Saxin, Tonya, Keisha, and April. April is the youngest. She was chosen as a mate for Robbie because she helped run the trade business. Also, her parents believed the other girls were too snobbish and would cause problems for Robbie.

After they agreed, the families planned the wedding ceremony quickly. April's parents were her only guests. Her sisters were away at school and did not return home for her wedding. Robbie's parents Lawrence and Benita Lockhart and one sister, Rita attended. April had always dreamed of a large wedding with all three of her sisters as bridesmaids and family from around the country in attendance. The parents wanted them to tie the knot quickly and decided to plan a lavish wedding once school was out for the summer. The lavish wedding never happened, and the newlyweds settled into life as husband and wife.

Robbie stood six feet two inches tall. He was light skinned with freckles and an oblong face. His hair was always cut low or sometimes he would sport a bald fade. All the girls loved him in school, the freckles weren't a turn off for he was very handsome. There were plenty of girls for him to date, but none captured his interest. He'd known April a long time and had deep feelings for her.

The relationship started out well. During the courting months and the first few years, they were inseparable. April couldn't quite pinpoint when Robbie changed. He became distant and cold. Even his family noticed, and no one knew what was going on with him.

The company hosted their annual summer banquet on a Friday evening. All of the employees and their families were attending. Prior to the event, tension between Robbie and April rose, as a deep, growing rift shook the foundation of the couple's relationship. Earlier that day they had an argument, which lasted about 15 minutes. Robbie wanted to take money out of the savings to make some purchases but refused to share what he was buying. The conversation got heated, and he stormed out of the house.

When Robbie arrived home, April was sitting at the bedroom mirror. He stood looking at her with disgust. After a minute or two, April could feel Robbie staring at her. She finally turned toward the door where he was standing and saw the frown on his face.

"What are you frowning at," she asked with concern?

Robbie took a deep breath. What he wanted to say wasn't easy, but necessary. "I can't do this anymore, April. I'm coming home to you every day, but I'm miserable." He stood with his hands in his pockets waiting for her response.

April couldn't believe her ears. Her husband was unhappy being with her. *How can that be?* "Wait! What?" She started shaking her head. "What are you saying?" Before she knew it, tears started rolling down her cheeks.

Robbie looked at his wife with disbelief. Surely, she had to know the marriage had to come to an end. They argued almost every day and they haven't spent any intimate time together in over a year. Her tears caused Robbie to pause for a moment. A part of him felt bad for her, but he could no longer delay. "April, you and I haven't been happy in a long time. Let's not prolong this any longer. I've moved on, and you need to do the same". The die has been cast, and there was no turning back.

"What do you mean that you've moved on," she exclaimed? Each word was followed with a sob. It was even hard for her to understand what she had spoken.

He shook his head. *Isn't it self-explanatory?* The words were in the forefront of his mind, but her reaction surprised him. All along he believed she shared the same sentiment. They haven't been getting along. Why should they stay together? "Don't act like you don't know what I'm talking about. We haven't been on the same page since...never really".

His words rung in her ears. It's true that they were arguing a lot more lately, but she thought that things could change with counseling and prayer. "Instead of working it out, you'd rather walk away," she asked? "Who is she?" That was the only logical explanation. In her heart, she knew there was another woman in the picture. Otherwise, he would try to work things out. As long as she's known him, he's never been one to quit unless another opportunity presented itself.

She picked up on what was happening. The words got stuck in his throat. It wasn't his plan for her to find out now. "It doesn't matter who, just know that it's over," Robbie retorted, turning toward the bathroom to avoid additional questions.

April jumped up and grabbed his left arm. "Don't you walk away from me," she cried, as tears ran steadily down her face. "You owe me an explanation."

"What difference does it make," he stated coldly. "I'm still divorcing you." Robbie removed her hand from his arm. If he revealed who he was in love with, all hades would break loose.

April started crying even harder. He was being secretive; it was someone she knew. "I'm going to ask you again, who is she or is it a he," she implored?

The last part of the question threw Robbie into a tailspin. *How could she possibly think that?* His blood pressure boiled; her accusation angered him. "What the heck are you saying?" His brows came close together, as he was trying to figure out what was going on in her mind.

"You know exactly what I'm saying," she shouted! "Why the secrecy? It's not like I won't find out, so you might as well tell me." The tears stopped rolling, as outrage took place of sorrow.

"You know I'm not gay," Robbie's voice elevated, as he towered over her.

"Apparently, I don't know anything," April replied. "I didn't see this coming. You can't do this to me, you can't!" She started bawling again.

Robbie was fed up. "You know you don't love me," he exclaimed. "We never really fell in love."

April cut him off. "Speak for yourself! I fell in love with you on our wedding day and have been in love with you ever since."

Her confession cut him deep, because he had no idea. When he started having feelings for his mistress, he told himself that April was losing interest in him. She stopped waiting for him at the door, and he figured she was ready to move on. Truth be told, he just wanted to justify his affair. Robbie shook his head and locked himself in the bathroom.

Although Robbie and April broke up more than two years ago, it was fresh in April's mind. As her thoughts returned to the present, April realized she'd learned a great deal from her marriage to Robbie and knew that she couldn't settle for less than unconditional love in her next relationship.

Later that evening, David and April spoke for more than two hours learning about each other's past and getting to know one another. They spoke in English and Turkish languages again. Both got a kick hearing the other speak the foreign language, and they taught one another new words and phrases.

Thoughts of April brought David joy. He was sorry to hear that she experienced infidelity in her first marriage. He's glad it didn't stop her from meeting him. She admitted that men approached her often, but she usually refused to engage with the opposite sex. He understood, because a part of him wanted to shut down from establishing any romantic relationships. While they spoke on the phone, David kept wondering what her plans were for the holiday. April's family was going out of town without her. It took a lot of effort for him to muster up enough nerve to ask her about her plans. She was spending the day with a co-worker.

They agreed to meet up the day after Christmas.

Chapter 11

Tiny flakes fell against the windshield of Joseph's Lincoln Navigator, as he cleaned the snow off the vehicle to prepare for the trek to Georgia for Christmas. Deloris was excited about seeing David and the twins. Gladys and Deloris were in close contact to keep each other informed with updates about their children. Tony and Ashley were finally adjusting to Damon being their father, but Dana still only acknowledged David as her father. Since she refused to consider him as her uncle, everyone believed that a reunion with David would help to ease the transition for her.

Deloris and Joseph led the caravan to Georgia. Micki was behind her parents, while Chris pulled up the rear. She leaned back in the plush, leather interior, recuperating from preparing for the long journey. The aroma of chicken wafted through the vehicle, as Joseph bit into a sandwich. He gripped the wheel with one strong hand, as the other placed the sandwich remains in a plastic container at his side. Jazz music permeated the automobile, and Deloris tapped her foot to the rhythm. Suddenly, her phone rang.

It was Micki on the line. She and her husband needed to stop for gas. The drive was about 13 hours, a straight shot down I-75. Whenever they headed down South, the family would make their first stop in Dayton, Ohio. They would gas up, take a restroom break, change drivers, and take care of whatever they needed to do before continuing the trip. Deloris always cooked for the long road trips to avoid spending money on food. This time, she made chicken salad sandwiches. Each vehicle had their own cooler to store the sandwiches and cold drinks.

Christmas was only two days away. The caravan started at midnight. If everything went well, they were expected to reach Gladys' home between two and three p.m. The travel plan included all the stops they would have to make during the trip.

Dana stayed on her phone talking to Nakita, Junior, and David. She missed her twin siblings and dad and couldn't wait to see them. Aunt Gladys was always a joy to be around, because she kept everyone laughing. This was going to be a fun, relaxing trip. Dana didn't have to worry about dealing with Damon. Nor did she have to be bored to death at Granddaddy Charles' home.

Secretly, she intended to stay in Georgia. Her mother figured she would try and only allowed her to take certain clothes. Dana didn't care. She knew her father could buy her new clothes.

However, she was concerned that David never answered her, when she asked if she could live with him and the twins. He always managed to steer the conversation in a different direction. Still, she was ecstatic that he agreed to allow her to visit.

Damon threatened to leave her mother alone to raise the three of them by herself. Although he had since apologized to her and her mother, he still didn't have Dana's respect. Further, she was disappointed in her mother for busting up the family. She detested the fact that Damon was her father.

Dana heard a beeping noise and noticed her phone's battery needed charging. Aunt Micki told her to hang up the phone, so she could charge it. Reluctantly, she said good-bye but would see her siblings soon enough. Her aunt tried to engage her in conversation, but Dana was not responsive. She figured Aunt Micki was trying to get inside her head. Dana didn't want to reveal anything she had planned. She only knew that she had to pull it off, because she couldn't stand to go back to Michigan.

After an hour of silence passed, Aunt Micki and her husband started a trivia game. Dana perked up, because she loved trivia and puzzles. For most of the trip, she answered questions about current events, the Bible, television shows, music, sports, animals, and geography. She also took a few naps in-between the games and gas stops. Before she knew it, the Campbell's caravan was crossing the Georgia state line.

Meanwhile, back in Michigan, Bernice was busy getting ready for her trip. She was used to traveling at least a couple times a year with Jackie's family, but all of that changed when she left David for Damon. The Campbell's were in Atlanta for the Christmas holiday, and she wanted to be with the twins for Christmas. She was busy packing and singing when she heard a knock at the door.

'Who could this be,' she thought to herself? Bernice lived in a secure building, and no one could enter unless they were buzzed in. Looking through the peephole, she saw Jackie, Damon, and the children were standing at the door. She was a little dismayed about their visit. Bernice opened the door and welcomed her family. She forced a smile, even though they showed up unexpectedly.

Everyone said "hello" as they piled into Bernice's place. Jackie and Damon sat together on the couch, with Tony and Ashley resting comfortably on the carpet. Bernice eased into the recliner.

"Well, what brings you guys here today and how did you get in without me buzzing you," she asked?

"The office manager recognized me and let us in," Jackie replied, getting up to look around the apartment. "Well, you've certainly made it cozy in here." Jackie stood smiling, as she surveyed her mother's new home.

Bernice moved into a senior citizen's residence. Her apartment was on the second floor. Walking into the apartment, visitors could hear the loud humming of her apartment-sized refrigerator. The kitchen was to the right of the front door. When Bernice opened the front door, visitors noticed sunlight filtering through the huge bay window in the living room. She'd closed the entrance to her bedroom.

"It's enough for me," Bernice replied, joining Jackie in looking around the living room. She turned to her daughter. "You never answered my question."

Jackie's eyebrows came together. "What question," she asked, as she sat down next to Damon?

"To what do I owe the pleasure of this visit," Bernice inquired, trotting back to her room to finish packing?

"Well Mama, it's two days before Christmas," Jackie raised her voice, so her mother could hear her in the bedroom. "I wanted to discuss what was on the menu."

Bernice walked back into the living room, folding a tan blouse. "I'm sure you two will think of something," she said softly.

A look of confusion clouded everyone's face. "What do you mean," Jackie asked? "Are you going somewhere?"

Bernice came back into the living room and stared at her daughter for a few seconds, before offering her one word, "Atlanta."

The children gawked at their grandmother, while Jackie's face fell.

"Bernice, the family has already left," Damon said. "They should be there already." He was sad that he wasn't welcome to visit his twin brother for Christmas.

"Oh, I wasn't planning to travel with them," she explained. "In October, David and I planned for me to fly to Atlanta." A satisfied look flashed across her face. She was disappointed in her daughter and wanted her to see the mistake she made in choosing Damon.

Jackie stood up. "You've had this planned since October, when were you going to tell me," she asked her mother?

"I thought I had told you, until you asked me what was on the Christmas dinner menu," she lied to her daughter. Bernice knew she hadn't said a word to Jackie.

"So, you're going to Atlanta to be with my family," Damon asked, getting madder by the minute?

"Yes, Jada and her boyfriend are driving me to the airport," Bernice replied. "As a matter of fact, they should be here any minute." Bernice walked back into her room to finish packing.

"Can I go too," Tony asked?

"I want to go," Ashley exclaimed!

"Oh, I'm sorry sweethearts, but I'm flying and we just can't purchase tickets that quickly without it costing a fortune."

"I'm sure Uncle David has the money," Ashley reasoned.

"Can you ask him for us, Mom?" Tony turned toward his mother for help. He had no idea that the two of them were not on speaking terms, unless it involved the twins and of late Dana.

"No one is going anywhere," Damon answered for Jackie. "Apparently, this is something your grandmother cooked up months ago."

"That's not fair," Tony cried, poking his lips out and scowling at the floor. "Why did Dana get to go? I guess I should have denied you as my father too."

"Yeah, she's been disrespectful and she gets to travel. You guys are mean." Ashley joined Tony with the crying.

They knew that Dana had been talking back to Jackie and Damon. When a child acted up in their family, a trip was usually out of the question.

Damon got out of his seat. "You let that child go on a trip, after the way she's been acting, and now Tony's questioning if he should call me Dad," Damon exclaimed dramatically, as he walked out the door.

Jada and her boyfriend were walking in the apartment, as Damon was leaving. She turned and looked at Damon, as he walked down the hall. "What's his problem," she asked?

As she walked in the room, she could see that Tony and Ashley were crying and Jackie had an angry expression on her face.

"What did I miss," Jada inquired?

"Oh nothing, I was just telling Jackie and the children that I won't be here for Christmas," Bernice explained. "Are we ready to go,"

Bernice asked Jada, as she walked into her bedroom to grab the suitcase? She wanted to leave before another argument broke out.

"I can't believe I have to cook for the holiday," Jackie complained, as everyone headed into the hallway.

"Well, that's usually what mothers do sweetie," Bernice informed Jackie with a smile. "I've always cooked for the holidays."

Bernice couldn't hide the smirk on her face. Jackie cooked breakfast and smaller meals. For events, she usually catered or the Campbell's shared the cooking duties with potluck meals all the time. *Cooking Christmas dinner will be a good experience for her*, Bernice thought.

Jackie noticed the smirk and knew that her mother was making fun of her. She was determined more than ever to prove her mother wrong. Jackie said goodbye to Jada and Bernice. She held the children's hands, as they walked toward the car. Damon peered at them through the windshield from inside the vehicle, where he sat by himself quietly sulking.

Chapter 12

In Georgia, the family gathered at Gladys' home. Deloris wanted to see her sister before the holiday. All of Gladys' children and grandchildren were there. David and the twins were the first to come out of the house. Deloris gave her son a warm hug, kissing his cheek affectionately. Joseph enclosed the twins in one big bear hug. Micki's eyes welled up with tears of joy at the sight of her brother, niece, and nephew. Dana ran straight to David, jumping into his arms. Chris and his family hugged David and the twins after everyone else's greeting.

The Campbell's marveled at Aunt Gladys' home. This was the first time they'd seen her newest house. She and her husband upgraded each time they moved. David and his cousins spent hours decorating the outside of the home with colorful lights and decorations, resulting in a breathtaking display.

Inside the home, the family spent time together eating and catching up with each other for hours. Gladys gave a tour of her home when they arrived, and she spent the rest of the evening entertaining her guests with hilarious stories about her childhood. Dana laughed so hard that she could hardly contain herself.

As a planner, David had worked out where everyone would sleep at his home. Micki and her husband decided to stay with Gladys. By early evening, Deloris was ready to go. David couldn't leave yet, because he had to pick up Bernice from the airport. Her flight was due in at 7 p.m. He hadn't told the family yet, because his mother wouldn't agree with her being here. He hoped she'd understand that he didn't want to deprive Bernice of spending time with the twins.

David pulled his mother to the side. "We can't leave yet," he said.

"Why not," she asked him? "You said we have about forty miles to travel, before we reach your home. We're all exhausted from the trip." Deloris had her hands on her hips, teasing her son.

David chuckled. He hesitated before he spoke. "I have to pick up Bernice from the airport," he explained, bracing himself for his mother's reaction.

Deloris stood with her mouth hung open. "Bernice is coming here," she exclaimed in surprise?

David explained to his mother that they worked out the deal a couple of months ago. She practically begged him to let her come see the twins for Christmas. He didn't want Bernice around him, but he decided it would be nice for the twins to have their maternal grandmother visit. She spent almost every holiday with his family. Her family rarely came together, so David included her in just about everything.

Deloris shrugged her shoulders after the explanation. She couldn't be mad at David. Bernice had every right to spend time with the children, because she was their grandmother also.

David was surprised his mother didn't blow up at him. She just nodded her head and walked away. It was supposed to be a surprise for the children. Dana didn't even know her maternal grandmother was coming to Atlanta. They would see Bernice, once he picked her up from the airport.

He thought about Damon's children. He missed Tony and Ashley too. There was a part of him that wanted one child to visit during Christmas break and another at spring break. He wouldn't keep them during summer break, because the twins will be home at that time. He'd already plotted in his mind, and he hoped Jackie agreed to allow him to spend time with the children he helped raise. As a reward, they could choose the child with the best grades to come for Christmas visits, since it was the longer break.

As the family shared stories with one another, David realized that it was time for him to pick up Bernice. His brother Chris rode with him for the quick trip. Aunt Gladys lived just eight minutes from the airport.

Bernice heard the airplanes taking off from where she stood in the arrivals area outside the airport. She knew David's black, luxury vehicle anywhere and waved to him from the curb. As he pulled up, she noticed Chris in the front seat. Chris used to like Jackie, until she betrayed his brother and Bernice was worried that he might not appreciate her presence. Surprisingly, Chris and David both exited the car to help Bernice with her bags.

However, Chris didn't know that Bernice wasn't just in Georgia to celebrate Christmas with the twins and Dana. She had a plan and hoped that her presence would help the family to forgive Jackie.

Upon arriving at his new home, David gave his master bedroom to his parents. He took Bernice's bags to Junior's room. The older girls, Dana and Nicole were sharing Nakita's room. David put himself in one of the guest bedrooms in the basement as well as for Chris and his family. Junior and Chris Jr. stayed upstairs with the girls and Bernice, they occupied the family room.

The twins and David were delighted that the family was there to visit. Everyone planned to stay until the 29th of December, but Bernice decided to stay after the New Year. It was a good thing to have an adult home, while the children were out of school on break. Bernice could spend time with them, while he worked.

David had a real Christmas tree set in the house, but it wasn't decorated yet. Deloris wanted to decorate the tree when she arrived. After helping decorate his aunt's house, David didn't have time. It was a fun, family project for tomorrow. Joseph and Deloris were so beat from the drive and the family fellowship earlier that they went straight to bed. David and Bernice still had enough energy to tend to all the children.

As joyful holiday music floated through his home, David asked the children to assist in decorating the rest of the house. It was a fun family project, and Bernice handed each child cookies to eat. The sugar rush gave the children more energy, and David was grateful for the help decorating. By the time his parents wake up in the morning, they'll only have to help decorate the tree.

110

When all the children were safely tucked into bed, David and Bernice sat up and talked for a while. She told David everything that was happening with Jackie, Damon, and the children. She even informed him of the argument that brewed just before she left. It saddened David that Ashley and Tony couldn't visit, but there was nothing he could do. His focus was on taking care of his two and possibly Dana. He still sent money to Jackie every month through his mother. She would purchase what the children needed instead of putting the money in Jackie's hands. Bernice told him that his financial support keeps Jackie afloat, and it definitely helped with the Christmas presents for this year.

David was relieved, when she explained that to him. He didn't want Ashley and Tony to suffer and didn't even get pleasure out of hearing about the challenges Damon and Jackie were experiencing. He could tell by the way Bernice was talking that she enjoyed watching her daughter struggle to care for her family. David wasn't pleased that she didn't bother to tell Jackie in advance about her visit to see the twins.

Suddenly, he regretted his decision to let Bernice come. It wasn't the twins she really wanted to see. Her desire was for Jackie to suffer for not staying married to him. David didn't want any part of her schemes. He politely bade her a good night and went to bed. As his head rested on the soft, luxury pillow, he couldn't help thinking about spending this first Christmas without his wife.

In the kitchen, Bernice could tell that David was upset after she spoke with him. She smiled, because she knew that he still cared for Jackie. His reaction confirmed it. If she kept showing Jackie what she was missing out on, maybe she would dump Damon and ask David to forgive her. If David kept hearing about Jackie's new life, maybe he'd realize just how much she means to him. Bernice's plan was right on target, and she had a feeling that it just might work.

Chapter 13

Jackie stared outside the kitchen patio door, watching each snowflake fall. A smile crept across her face, as she sipped coffee from a colorful holiday cup. Snow blanketed the backyard and neighboring rooftops, forming icicles around the edges. Like decorative frost reaching for the ground, the beautiful snow and ice fairyland highlighted the season. She relished the white Christmas, a scene so beautiful that it took her breath away. Later she would enjoy a snowball fight, build a snowman, and make snow angels with her children and Damon. She couldn't wait for the day to unfold. She hated that the older three weren't present. *Oh, how she missed them so!*

This was her first Christmas without David, Dana, and the twins. Even her mother joined the Campbell family in Georgia for Christmas. *Focus on the good*, she reminded herself. Jackie loved the fact that she and Damon were spending the holiday together. She'd do everything to make this day a peaceful one and said a silent prayer to herself.

At that moment, Tony came into the kitchen and hugged her. "I know you're sad Mama, but it'll get better," he comforted her, flashing a big smile.

Jackie smiled in response, her son's kindness and words of encouragement warmed her heart. Despite the small number of gifts he received, Tony exuded optimism and joy. Jackie put her arm around her son, and the two stood together hugging one another at the patio door. Tony's eyes followed his mother's gaze to the winter wonderland outside, which showcased pure, falling snow against the backdrop of blue sky. On the horizon, the sun continued to rise, shining brightly through the early morning gusts of wind, which swirled layers of snow from yard to yard.

"Come on Mama," Tony said, pulling her away from the door toward the living room. Jackie willingly joined the rest of the family.

It wasn't a usual Christmas for them. Tony and Ashley only received a few gifts this year. If it weren't for David's financial support, there wouldn't be any gifts, except for what the grandparents had given. David's money also helped buy food for the day. Jackie and Damon thought Bernice would help them buy the Christmas food, but she was in Georgia.

They didn't pull names with the rest of the family this year, because they weren't able to purchase extra gifts. However, the family supported them by giving them money for other expenses, so they were grateful for the help.

Jackie could see Tony making the most of his few gifts. Ashley also showed her gratitude. It was quite a change from previous Christmas celebrations. They usually received everything they wanted. Yesterday evening, Damon gave them a pep talk, encouraging both to be grateful for what they have and reminding them that there were a lot of children who had less.

Damon and his parents talked Micki into letting Jackie stay in her mother's home. They even asked her to be a little lenient on the rent amount, considering the children were family and needed to be in a good location. Micki wasn't too happy with the request, but she changed her mind for the sake of the children. She wanted Jackie and Damon to suffer, but she figured Dana was giving them enough trouble with her disrespectful behavior.

Adjusting to the new life without David and the twins wasn't easy. Prior to the holiday, Damon hadn't seen Jackie or the children for a few weeks. He was embarrassed by all that had transpired. The children no longer adored him like they did when he was just 'Uncle Damon'. He couldn't give them the same lifestyle David provided. As a result, Jackie bombarded his phone with text messages, asking for his help with the children.

He came to Jackie's home for Christmas mainly to spend time with his son and daughter. The three of them were bonding. Damon wasn't sure that he would be a good father, because David set such a high bar.

A nagging feeling enveloped Jackie's mind, because Damon was distancing himself from his relationship with her. She suspected that he was not all in, and the distance between them for the last two weeks concerned her. Prior to his disappearing act, Damon often went out by himself and stayed away for long periods of time. If she called him, he returned her call hours later. His behavior was very different from David's constant and dependable presence.

It was hard not to compare Damon and David. Her mind wandered back to Christmas celebrations of the past. On their first Christmas together, David gave her a new car, pearl jewelry, her favorite perfume, five outfits, and ordered a catered dinner. As the years progressed, she enjoyed all the economic benefits of the life she shared with David. Perhaps she took his wealth and his love for granted.

Ashley, Tony, and Damon played with the toys, but Jackie's mind was not fully present. Her lips curved up slightly into a smile, as her thoughts lingered in the past. She remembered the twins' first Christmas. They were only six months old. David brought home just about every toy on the market for a baby. It was too much, and they ended up giving some of it away. He did the same thing for Dana. By her third pregnancy, she spoke with David about not purchasing every baby toy in the store for Ashley.

An enticing aroma brought Jackie back to the present. Suddenly, she realized she needed to tend to the food she was cooking in the kitchen. Releasing her memories, Jackie stood up to check on the food. They were having the usual Christmas dinner with turkey, dressing, yams, macaroni and cheese, rolls, potato salad, and apple pie for dessert.

Damon followed Jackie into the kitchen. "I couldn't help but notice that your mind was elsewhere," he said flatly.

She grinned. "I was thinking of past holidays and missing the rest of my family," she replied, opening the oven door to baste the turkey.

"You were thinking about David," Damon responded. It was more of a statement than a question. Damon leaned against the counter and folded his arms. He didn't blame her for thinking about David, after all Damon and Jackie's relationship was on rocky ground. *'I came to the house for Ashley and Tony, not for Jackie anyway,'* Damon reminded himself.

"Damon, you don't have to be upset, because I'm not longing for David or anything like that," she replied, affectionately touching his cheek with the palm of her hand.

"What are you longing for," he asked her playfully, encircling her in his muscular arms for a hug.

She rested her head on his chest, hearing his measured breaths and smelling Damon's fragrant cologne. Jackie didn't answer right away. "I'm just missing how Christmas used to be," Jackie answered honestly.

Damon's tone confused her, because he acted like he didn't care that she was not fully in the moment. Suddenly, Damon released Jackie and stepped away from the hug. He confronted her with his true feelings.

"I know I didn't deliver like my brother has always done," Damon's eyes looked to the floor and then into Jackie's eyes, silently pleading for her approval. He'd promised her the world, when she was married to his brother. However, confronted with the opportunity, he was painfully aware that he'd fallen short.

"I'm not upset," she said, moving toward him and gently encircling his waist with her arms. "I am very happy sharing the day with you, and I am looking forward to spending every Christmas with you." She playfully shook him around the hips and smiled to ease his mind.

"You're not upset that we didn't buy gifts for one another," Damon asked, fearful of her answer?

"Of course not," Jackie replied. "We both agreed we would skip this year, but next year will be different." She moved her face closer to his, gingerly placing a kiss on his lips.

Damon lifted Jackie into a bear hug, holding her close. A few moments later, Ashley interrupted them.

"Can we eat breakfast now, 'cause I'm starving," she asked, with a huge grin on her face?

Damon and Jackie looked at each other with a smile.

"Pancakes and bacon coming up," Damon said, giving Jackie a peck on the cheek before moving toward the refrigerator to cook breakfast. Ashley followed him to help, and Jackie retreated to the living room, giving Damon time with Ashley to enjoy his first Christmas as her father.

As she sank into the comfortable sofa, Jackie's mind returned to her Christmas memories.

16 Years Ago...

Georgia

The Campbell family arrived back at Aunt Gladys' home around noon. David wanted to pick Jackie up and have her ride with him and the family, but she declined. So, he asked her to come around 12:30 p.m. He hoped everything would be set up, before she arrived.

The house was festive with decorations throughout each room. Strands of multicolored lights adorned wooden accents and lit room entrances. A green, artificial tree nearly reached the living room's ceiling, decorated with gold ornaments, red lights, and wallet-sized pictures of the children, which were encased in white paper frames with miniature, red bows.

Each family bought two gifts for those whose name they had drawn, giving a present to the adults and one for the children. Relatives stacked presents under the tree, offering one another a wide array of gifts with seasonal wrappings. Christmas music floated through the air, and the family sang along to Silent Night, Joy to the World, and other popular songs.

At noon, the doorbell rang. David knew it was Jackie, and he moved quickly toward the front entrance, wanting to be the first to greet her. As he opened the door, Jackie's radiating beauty dazzled him. She stood confidently in the doorway, looking sophisticated in black slacks and a black jacket. Her hair was dyed an auburn color, hanging down her back in a wavy style.

David stood still for a moment, admiring her beauty. "You look great," he complimented her with enthusiasm!

Jackie offered him a confident smile, which contrast her feelings, as nervousness threatened to overwhelm her. "Thank you, David; so do you," she replied.

She walked through the doors into his welcome embrace, and David's senses noted every intoxicating detail about Jackie, from the warm embrace to the fresh scent of her lavender bath wash.

"Come on, I've told the family you were coming," he explained with happiness evident on his face. "This is my aunt's house." He was rambling, and nervous energy caused him to talk excessively.

Gently taking her hand, David guided Jackie into the living room to meet his family. She felt David's pulse rate increase in the excitement of the moment.

"Hey everybody, I would like to introduce you to Jackie," David announced, introducing her to each family member.

Damon walked up to David smiling. "Wow, no wonder you were all smiles this morning," he whispered jokingly, giving his brother a congratulatory pat on the back while leaning toward his ear. At that moment, David realized that he and Jackie were still holding hands.

They were officially a couple. He looked into her beautiful hazel, brown eyes and noticed a gleam of acceptance and joy. She turned her head away when their eyes met. It was the first time she'd felt this strongly about David, as butterflies briefly moved across her stomach.

Deloris watched the interaction curiously, patting the seat beside her for Jackie to sit down. "David," his mother's voice rang out over the elevated voices of family members in the room. "Go help your father bring in the rest of the presents, while I get to know Jackie."

David looked at Jackie, as if asking her permission. She nodded her head, while Damon put both of his hands on David's shoulders, walking him toward the foyer and out of the house to help Joseph.

Deloris had heard quite a bit about Jackie. David did not over exaggerate her beauty. She had a majestic air and a confidence, which drew all eyes in the room to her, as if she were the focal point. Deloris made it a point to make her as comfortable as possible, because she knew how much Jackie meant to her son. As she walked toward the sofa, Deloris stood and hugged her warmly. She took her hand, as they sat together laughing and joking with each other.

The food was ready by the time David returned from helping his father. Family members prepared to feast on turkey, dressing, fried chicken, honey baked ham, collard greens, macaroni and cheese, potato salad, coleslaw, yams, cornbread, and dinner rolls. For dessert, mouth-watering sweet potato pies, a punch bowl cake, and peach cobbler awaited them. Gladys was known best for her scrumptious cobblers, and Deloris had made a special request.

As David entered the living room, he walked directly toward Jackie, holding her hand in his as the family gathered for prayer. Everyone held hands, and Joseph said the blessing, thanking God for family, fellowship, and food. After the blessing, the children were served first. As David's guest, Jackie was next at Gladys' request.

Jackie felt the warmth and love from the Campbell family. David's hand brushed the small of her back, as she fixed two plates. Tables and chairs were set up throughout the home to accommodate family members and guests. Jackie and David settled on a spot near Damon in the family room.

The two of them were eating, when Micki started the conversation. "The young woman with the dark hair, is she your sister," she asked, with an inquisitive look?

The question made David a little uneasy, because his sister Micki was very opinionated and rarely liked girls, which he invited home. He smiled at Jackie. "Yes, she's my sister," he replied softly.

Jackie pondered over his response. "I don't think she likes me very much," she responded quietly, leaning in to whisper in his ear. "You should have seen the mean looks she was giving me." David pursed his lips together, hoping Micki was not starting any drama.

David chuckled. "You need not worry about Micki," he replied. "She'll come around in her own time." He gave her a reassuring look to ease her discomfort, because he noticed Micki roll her eyes at Jackie from across the room.

Jackie shrugged her shoulders. "If you say so, but maybe I should stay clear of her, so that I'm not offending her in any way," Jackie responded. There was concern in her voice. The last thing she wanted to do was cause tension among the family, especially since Deloris had been so kind and welcoming.

"I would, if I were you," David chuckled again, giving her a playful smile.

She laughed at his response. They spent the rest of the time enjoying each other's company and joking with Damon, who'd joked with them while they ate. Joseph came in the room and sat next to Jackie, wanting to get to know her better.

Everyone was having a good time it seemed, except Micki. Deloris purposely sought her out to find out what was wrong. It wasn't like her to go off by herself, unless she was upset.

She found her in the garage and sat next to her, looking out of the open garage door at the children playing in the front yard. "Why are you over here in the corner, secluded from the rest of the family," Deloris asked Micki, looking her dead in the eye?

Micki shrugged. "Just thinking," she responded. She paused and asked the burning question that's been in her mind since this afternoon. "Who is that young woman David invited," she inquired?

Deloris smiled, as Jackie's beautiful face came into her mind. "Oh, that's Jackie, a friend of David's apparently."

Micki looked at Deloris confused. "David never mentioned to me that he had a new girlfriend," Micki complained.

Deloris leaned back some. "Well, it was bound to happen sooner or later," she said. "Surely, you didn't expect him to stay single the rest of his life," she asked a rhetorical question?

David had always been there for Micki, and she couldn't bear the thought of losing him permanently. Micki saw Jackie as a threat to the close relationship she had with her brother. David had never mentioned that he was seeing someone. Plus, there was something about her that Micki couldn't quite put her finger on. She decided that she just didn't like David's new girlfriend.

Why couldn't Jackie have met Damon instead? Damon was a playboy, jumping from one relationship to another. He'd probably never commit to anyone. However, it didn't matter to Micki, because Damon didn't care for her the way David did.

"I don't like her," Micki announced to her mother emphatically.

"Oh Micki, we need to support David's relationship," Deloris implored of her daughter. "He really likes her. "

Damon came into the garage and sat next to Micki. He spoke softly and gently, "I know what you're doing."

Micki jerked her head toward Damon. "What are you talking about," she retorted?

Damon smiled at Micki, because he didn't want to start an argument but wanted her to know she was up to no good. "When you first walked through the door, you made it your task to mix and mingle with everyone, until Jackie showed up. Your whole demeanor changed, and everyone noticed it."

Micki turned her head toward the wall. "You're imagining things," she replied, surprised her feelings were so transparent to the family.

Deloris took Micki's hand. "I know your brother has taken care of you over the years, but it's time to let him go build his own family."

She shot her response back. "I have let it go," Micki replied, her head still turned.

"No, you haven't," Deloris rubbed Micki's back. "You're in the garage sulking over what may come." There was no response. Deloris took Micki's silence as affirmation, and she stood up to leave.

Micki turned toward Damon and her mother. "You shouldn't accuse people of things you know nothing about," Micki replied. "I'm telling you something is not right about that woman." She did everything she could to hide her resentment and to sound innocent.

Damon responded angrily. "What you need to realize is *that woman* is David's choice," he said. "It's a decision that he has to live with, so suck it up and come rejoin the family." Deloris nodded in agreement and hurriedly left the garage, when she heard more guests arriving inside the house.

Micki looked defeated, knowing that her relationship with her brother David was never going to be the same. She wandered back into the house, eyeing Jackie curiously from a distance.

Jackie noticed Micki's eyes following her around the house, as she greeted relatives. David stayed at her side with his arm draped around her shoulders or his hand gently caressing the small of her back, as if he couldn't bear to stand so close without touching her.

Micki sniffed in disapproval, when she overheard David invite Jackie to spend the next day with the family.

David was relieved that she'd accepted the invitation, because he thought Micki's behavior might dissuade Jackie. He couldn't wait to see her again tomorrow. The couple said goodbye in front of her mid-sized sedan and hugged each other. Upon returning, Micki looked at him accusingly.

"David," Micki said, standing in the living room where everyone had gathered.

"Yes, my dear," David replied, still floating on air from the wonderful day with Jackie and the family.

She looked around the room, as if she were searching for something. "Where is my present," Micki asked? Normally, David gave her a separate gift in addition to the gifts she received from her assigned family member. However, in his excitement over Jackie, he'd forgotten.

Everyone stopped what they were doing. All eyes fell on Micki.

Micki looked at everyone, as they gawked at her.

"Son," Joseph nudged David, while he was sitting next to him.

"I'm on it, Dad," David said, grabbing Micki by the hand. They went into the dining room, as he spoke to her gently about how much he loved her.

As they were leaving the room, Micki could hear whispers amongst the family. Someone whispered, '*I knew she was going to act out.*'

"David, what's going on," she asked, concerned that something had happened to her present from him?

David gave her a smile and took a deep breath. "I didn't get a separate gift for you this year," he explained. "Still, I want you to know how much you mean to me."

Micki sucked her teeth and looked away, realizing that things were already different. Jackie was going to come into the family and change everything. Micki knew it was only a matter of time before David and Jackie were married, because she'd never seen her brother act like that around any other woman.

"Oh, come here," David chuckled, hugging his sister closely, as a small frown covered her face. "Stop being melodramatic," he chided her. "Tell you what, we'll go shopping together soon, just you and me."

Micki smiled, vowing to herself not to tell David that she didn't like Jackie. They made their way back to the family just in time to hear Aunt Gladys crack a joke, which sent everyone into fits of laughter.

Chapter 14

In the present...

Georgia

"Dad," where are my presents," Dana asked, as she looked underneath the tree at Aunt Gladys' house for the third time? David experienced a déjà vu moment, as he looked into his daughter Dana's eyes, realizing how much she reminded him of his sister Micki. He gently took her hand and quietly led her away from the family into the office to talk.

David took his time answering her. "As you know, Damon and your mother were against you coming," he responded.

Dana scoffed, "Yeah, I know, but what does that have to do with anything?"

David sighed. "Well, it was everyone actually who didn't want you to come, but I talked them into bringing you down here." His heart was broken, because he didn't want to tell Dana that she wasn't getting any presents. It was unfair that Jackie and Damon didn't let her know about the agreement, before she left Michigan.

"Just spill it, Dad," Dana exclaimed.

"Ok, in order to get you down here, there was a contingency agreement with your mother and Damon," he explained. "I agreed that you'd receive no Christmas gifts because of your behavior." There, he'd said it.

"What!" Dana exclaimed, standing up from her seat, as anger boiled inside of her. She couldn't believe her family didn't buy her any presents after all they'd been through.

David gently touched her on her shoulder to ease her back to her seat. He leaned toward her with his hands folded in front of him.

Tears slid down Dana's face. "Why didn't anyone tell me," she cried?

David felt helpless, and he hated to see Dana crying. He looked down at the floor, before he spoke again. Dana's face turned red and tears flowed down her face like a stream. He could see the hurt and disappointment in her eyes.

"I'm sorry, honey," David comforted her gently. "I assumed your mother had already spoken with you about the agreement."

"She didn't tell me anything," she shook her head. "This is way beyond a punishment; this is torture!" Her mind went racing about the recent events that had taken place, prior to David and the twins moving to Georgia. Tony almost died, her mother was cheating on her father, and the man she has known as her dad was not her father after all. David was literally her uncle.

David pursed his lips. "I know this comes as a shock to you, but it was the only card I had left to play to get your mother to agree."

"Why was she so against it," Dana snapped at her father? The torment of not receiving one gift was mind boggling.

"Well, your blatant disrespect for your mother and Damon was why she was against it," he replied.

"Disrespect!" Dana exclaimed. "But it's alright for them to be disrespectful to you and all us kids?"

She couldn't believe her father had agreed to such an arrangement, after all the times she defended her father to her mother. "How could you do this to me dad?" Dana asked, dramatically folding her arms on the table and placing her head face down on top of her arms. The crying started again.

"Honey, I raised you better than to speak to your elders in the way that you spoke to Jackie and Damon," David responded in a firm tone. "Remember what we learned in church about right thinking followed by right action?"

By the time the last word left David's lips, Dana was shaking uncontrollably. There was a break in her speech, as she spoke. "They shouldn't have done what they did, Dad," she sobbed. With sadness in her eyes, Dana was pleading her case. It wasn't right that the adults got to make awful decisions and the children suffer for it. She and her siblings were the victims in this situation, only she was bold enough to speak against it.

"I'm just saying what everyone else is afraid to say," she explained. "They're wrong, Dad! Why am I being punished for what they did?"

David reached for her hands again. "It's alright to speak your mind, but there's a right way and a wrong way to do it," David advised. "You chose the wrong way. Just like I chose the wrong way to express my anger at Damon by hitting him at the hospital. Even though I felt he deserved it, I still had to pay for the consequences of my actions."

Dana thought about that day when he and Uncle Damon went to jail. Dana wiped her face with her sleeve. She reconciled herself to the fact that she had to take responsibility for her actions. She mumbled her words. "I hate this," she sighed in exasperation.

"I hate it even more," David agreed, hugging her closely.

"If I apologize, may I receive my gifts then," Dana asked hopefully.

"You mean *when* you apologize, and your gift was a chance to come visit with the family in Georgia."

"I wished she would've told me," Dana sighed. "I would have stayed home."

"If I know Damon, you probably wouldn't have received anything there either," David chuckled.

She slid the chair back in frustration. "This isn't fair, Dad," Dana screamed, running out of the room and into a bedroom upstairs. Everyone could hear the door slam.

David sat at the table shaking his head.

His mother came into the office. "Do you want me to go after her," she asked? His parents always had a hand in disciplining their grandchildren. Slamming doors in the Campbell family was unacceptable behavior. His parents didn't tolerate back talk, like Dana had just done.

"No Mama, I'll let her calm down," David replied. "After all, she did just find out that she's getting no presents this year."

David called to the twins. If he wanted the children to respect their mother, he'd have to make sure that they did so. "Call your mother and siblings," he instructed, as Junior and Nakita curiously poked their heads into the room. Deloris nodded in agreement, following the children into the hallway to make sure that they dialed the number immediately.

In the present...

Michigan

Damon heard the phone ring in the living room at the same time that he felt the cellular phone vibrate in his pants' pocket. He smiled at Tony, who was piling dinner onto his plate a few feet away. Tony had to admit to himself that his mom had made a feast for the four of them.

Jackie answered her cell phone, as she gave the gravy one last stir. Clicking the speaker phone button, she listened intently while pouring the thick, brown liquid from the pot into a gravy boat on the counter.

"Merry Christmas, Mom," Junior said, his changing voice squeaking slightly. Hearing the sound of her oldest son's voice caused a smile to make its way across her face.

"Hi, Junior," she said, accentuating his name in her excitement.

"Hi, Junior," Ashley and Tony spoke simultaneously from the table, hoping that their voices carried far enough for their brother to hear them. Since they could all hear one another with the phone's speaker, Junior, Nakita, Jackie, Ashley and Tony exchanged stories and shared details about their respective Christmas experiences for several minutes.

Damon watched for a moment before walking into the living room. Taking out his cellphone, he sent a short response to the text he received. It read, *'7 p.m. '*. He returned to the kitchen, just as Jackie beckoned for him to lead a Christmas prayer with them over the phone.

After finishing the conversation with the twins, Tony and Ashley consumed the food, relishing every morsel. Their mother had never cooked a full Christmas dinner alone, and they didn't know that she could do it. Damon leaned forward slightly in his seat to gently take Jackie's hand in his own. "That was fantastic," he commented, causing her cheeks to turn a slight rose color.

Standing up from the table, Damon rubbed Tony on the top of his head, gave Ashley a light squeeze on her cheek and explained that he needed to drop off presents to some friends. He was only being partially honest and noticed both children's body slump slightly at his announcement. He didn't want to ruin Christmas, but he had other commitments.

Jackie couldn't believe her ears. She'd given up her entire family for this man, and he couldn't commit to spending a full holiday with them. She slowly began to clear the table, refusing to ruin Ashley and Tony's Christmas by arguing with Damon. Flashing a bright smile, she offered them another serving of apple pie. It was Aunt Gladys' recipe, and Tony smiled in return.

'Apple pie makes everything better, ' Jackie thought to herself, as she fixed herself and the children each a heaping portion with ice cream on top. She raised an eyebrow at Damon and waved to him dismissively.

Damon stepped out of the warm, comfortable home into the cold weather, trudging through the snow toward his ride. He and Jackie weren't going to work out, he decided. In all the years he's known her, she has never acted so possessive. Each day they spend together, she became clingier. It's like she doesn't have a mind of her own. He didn't see it before, and she's never portrayed that side of herself. It was probably because David was in the picture.

He wanted to give her an ultimatum, but it wasn't needed. Jackie sent him a barrage of text messages, attacking his decision making and character. The messages flooded his cell phone, until he finally turned it off. He didn't deserve that from her, nor was he going to take it.

All the sneaking around they did for so many years and wishing for them to be together came to naught. Their relationship would not flourish. He broke his brother's heart for nothing. Insecure and clingy women were not his cup of tea. He wanted someone that trusted him and that he could also trust. '*Bridget is that type of lady,*' he said to himself, thinking about the kind and loving text she sent him earlier. It was naïve of Jackie to believe that in the years that she'd been married to David that he'd been committed only to her. He enjoyed the freedom of getting to know many women. Something about Bridget was different though.

He'd never committed to Bridget, because he thought he may love Jackie. Unfortunately, six months after everyone found out about their secret affair, the two spent more time fighting than anything else. People don't fall out of love that quickly. Maybe he wanted her, because she belonged to someone else. Perhaps the thrill and intensity of a secret romance kept his interest. Of late, his interest in Jackie had waned significantly.

In addition, there was the matter of the children. He loves them, but hates the weight of all the responsibility. There was no denying that David wasn't the father. However, maybe he wasn't Dana nor Ashley's father either. A part of him hoped that was the case. The problem was he didn't have the money to get the test done. Damon thought to ask his parents. Any money they gave him went directly to things for the children. They refuse to put money directly in his hands a long time ago.

His friend Phil's words came rushing back to his memory. *'Don't put your name on those birth certificates, until you are sure the children belong to you,'* Phil told him. Damon and Jackie took David's name off, because Damon wanted to get even with him for jumping him at the hospital. It was a dumb decision. He should have listened to Phil. If he would have left well enough alone, David would be on the hook to pay child support. Feelings of regret overwhelmed him. There was no way he could survive on his income and care for these children by himself.

It was probably best that Dana was with David for the holiday. She always considered Damon's brother as her father anyway. Damon knew her nasty attitude was fueled by her own anger and hurt over her family breaking up. Dana may never accept him as her father, and he was ok with that.

As he drove quietly through the city streets, Damon's thoughts shifted to his twin brother. He missed David and hated that he did this to him. They'd always been close, and he prayed that his brother would someday forgive him. Every morning, he prayed earnestly for David. Even though Damon didn't feel worthy of God's love, he knew that David was worthy of it. He prayed that his brother could find a woman that loved him the way he deserved. Jackie loved David, but her deception dishonored their family. A part of Damon blamed Jackie for allowing him to seduce her. It wasn't right of them to mislead David all those years. If the tables were turned, he probably would have killed his brother. Feelings of guilt permeated Damon's thoughts. If David never forgave him, he wouldn't hold it against him.

A part of him was glad David found out about Jackie. In the aftermath, Damon realized that he and Jackie are not a good match, leaving him free to move forward in his life. David was also free from her, instead of constantly working hard to please a woman who was sleeping with his brother.

Memories came back to Damon's mind as he thought of all the things his brother had done for his wife. If she saw something that she wanted, he would buy it for her. He made elaborate plans for the family, giving them unforgettable experiences. No task was too small or too big, if it meant making David's family happy. Jackie seemed happy when he did all those things, but she often went back to her melancholy state. *'It would be nice if Jackie learned how to appreciate the beauty of gifts, instead of always wanting and expecting more from everyone,'* Damon thought.

Damon arrived at Bridget's home and rang the doorbell. She opened the door with a welcoming smile. In her arms, she held a 4-month-old baby. Damon carefully hugged Bridget and took his baby son Dominique into his arms.

"Merry Christmas little one," he cooed, carrying him through the living room cluttered with baby toys to sit on the couch. Bridget sat beside Damon, happy that he'd finally arrived.

She and Dominique lived in a housing project in Hamtramck, a city near Detroit. Their dwelling place was located on the service drive off interstate 75. The bottom level consisted of a living room, kitchen, and utility room. Upstairs, a modern three-bedroom and one-bath configuration gave the couple plenty of room for the new baby. Surprisingly, the low-income housing units were exceptionally well made, with up-to-date appliances and aesthetically pleasing finishes. With decorative tile flooring on the bottom level and hardwood floors upstairs, Bridget's place was cozy and comfortable.

Bridget wanted to know, if he was going to introduce his son to the Campbell family. Damon told her that his family was out of town for the holiday but was due back in four days. Months ago, he told Bridget about the affair with Jackie and his brother's departure to Atlanta. He appreciated that she did not criticize or pressure him to decide between her and Jackie.

What Damon didn't know was that every morning Bridget arose, studying scriptures, and praying for God to help Damon resolve his entanglements. She wanted to have a family with him. She'd made mistakes in her life, but she knew that she was forgiven. There is no condemnation in Christ, only forgiveness. She'd joined a church in the neighborhood and earnestly prayed for herself and her new family.

Time was slipping away, as they continued to talk and play with little Dominique. Since Dominique was too young to play outside in the snow, the couple chose a child-friendly movie to watch on television. He found a peace with Bridget, which was missing with Jackie. It was like she had very few expectations of him, which made him want to give her more. She nodded off to sleep on the couch beside him. He watched her face, etching every detail in his mind. Their son had her smooth, caramel-colored complexion and full lips. A twinge of guilt hit him again, because he wished that he could be fully present with her and his new family. His past choices hindered him from moving forward.

Sighing deeply, Damon looked down at his sleeping son, a tiny replica of himself. *'What have I ever done to deserve such a gift,'* he asked himself?

Later that night, Damon drove back to Bloomfield Hills. He thought of the question Ashley asked him, while they were cooking breakfast. She wanted to know when Damon and Jackie were going to get married. He didn't know where Ashley got that idea. The discussion of marriage never came up with his daughter. It's possible that she overheard Jackie speaking with someone about it. Damon didn't know how to answer the question, so he changed the subject. He'd thought of marrying Jackie, but the origin of their relationship and his feelings for Bridget kept him from speaking with her about it. He knew the time was coming, when he'd have to make a definite choice between the two of them.

When Damon pulled into Jackie's driveway, she was standing at the door with her arms folded. He could tell by the look on her face that she was angry. Damon had barely stepped out of the vehicle, before he was blown away by her attack. Jackie had walked down the steps to meet him by his car. Her hand hit him so forcefully in the face that he fell backward against the vehicle. She told him he was unfaithful, and he was a liar. He really didn't hear much of what she said, because he was still reeling from the slap. Damon stood up. "I can't believe you just hit me," he exclaimed.

"It serves you right," Jackie was screaming to the top of her lungs!

"You're a crazy broad, and I don't have to take this from you," Damon shouted, wishing that he'd never left Bridget's home.

"Where do you think you're going," Jackie asked?

"Away from you, away from here," Damon responded in a calmer tone.

"Don't you walk away from me," Jackie said, grabbing his arm.

Damon looked back at her, as his right foot stepped into the vehicle. Before he sat in the seat, he saw Tony and Ashley staring at him from an upstairs window. He gave them a half smile, and then closed the door to his car to return to Dominique and Bridget.

Jackie stood alone, with her hands on her head crying.

In the present...

Georgia

Early the next morning, the Campbell family arose to cook breakfast, dress, and head out to tour Atlanta. They took a similar tour, whenever the family spent the holidays at Aunt Gladys' home. This was the first year in a long time that Jackie was not with them. Deloris offered to stay behind to help cook dinner, a task Jackie and her mother Bernice usually tackled together the day after the holiday. She planned to cook a seafood gumbo. Dana had to stay back as part of her punishment, so she also offered to help.

David was waiting for April to arrive. They'd spent a lot of time talking on the phone after the mall encounter. April arrived at the house around 10 a.m. She looked even more stunning than usual. She pulled her dark, flowing mane into a ponytail, which accentuated her lovely eyes. She looked around, as she entered

David's new home. "This is your house," April asked, amazed at the massive size of the living room and kitchen?

"Yes, it is," David replied. "Come on, I'll give you a tour." David showed her around the house, introducing her to family members, as they moved from room to room.

Bernice spoke to April but was a little standoffish. April's presence bothered her to the core. David told her two nights ago that he wasn't dating anyone. From what she could tell, this was April's first time in David's house. Bernice was not going to let a new woman stop her plans for David and Jackie's reconciliation.

Something Gladys told her the day before came to her mind. *David has moved on with his life.* It suddenly dawned on her that it was useless for her to be here. David hadn't asked her once about Jackie. He asked about the children, but it was Bernice who volunteered the information about her daughter. He showed a lack of interest. David may not be dating April as of yet, but from the way they were acting toward each other, a courtship wasn't far off.

Bernice wasn't ready to give up just yet. Jackie and David had been married for 15 years, and that was long enough for them to work out their differences and mend the relationship. She just didn't want Jackie to throw it all away.

After David gave April a tour of the home, he led everyone outside on the way to tour Atlanta. This was her time to pry information from Deloris. First, she sent Jackie a text telling her about David and April. Even though her plan seemed hopeless, she remained optimistic.

Last night, she'd thought about cutting her trip short but was glad she didn't. April's appearance was a surprising development. The original plan was to fly back home after the new year. With an open ticket, she was able to leave when she chose, unless David put her out before that time. The rest of the family was leaving on the 29th. A plan formed in her mind, as she thought of ways to bring David back to Jackie. A devious smile appeared across her face.

"What are you smiling about," Deloris asked with a curious, accusatory look on her face?

Bernice was startled when Deloris spoke. "Oh nothing," she said, sitting at the kitchen table with her coffee cup in both hands. "I'm so glad that I am able to still spend time with you all." She gave Deloris a sheepish grin.

"We're glad you could come," Deloris replied. "The twins and Dana need you."

They worked quietly for a moment with gospel music playing in the background. Bernice couldn't contain herself any longer. "Hey, what do you think of April," she asked Deloris? Deloris was smiling as she came to join Bernice at the table.

"She's a nice girl," Deloris replied. "I'm glad David has someone to take his mind off of everything."

Bernice's face dropped. The statement caught her off guard. It was a long shot to think that Deloris shared her same sentiment that David was moving too fast. "David told me that they aren't dating," Bernice responded. She tried to sound polite as possible, but inside her emotions were unraveling.

"Yes, I know... but I'm just glad there is someone here to help him smile," Deloris responded. This was her chance to let Bernice know that she and her family approved of April. Gladys told her about her suspicion that Bernice came to Georgia to try to get David and Jackie back together. The sisters surmised that without Deloris' son in her life, Bernice couldn't travel or get extra money. Even though Bernice had enough to live on, she still received help from David. He cared for her, as if she were his own mother. She admired her son for his kindness, but always felt Bernice was undeserving with her conniving and manipulative ways.

Bernice had to gather her composure, but her emotions displayed her true feelings. Deloris is happy for her son. It wouldn't be wise for Bernice to show unhappiness and blow her cover.

135

"So, what's the plan while the others are away," she asked Deloris?

"We are going to cook the gumbo, remember," Deloris chuckled.

"Oh, that's right," Bernice giggled, in contrast to the turmoil within her mind. "What do you need me to do?"

Deloris asked Bernice to cut up vegetables, and yelled for Dana to come in the kitchen to help. As she cut up the veggies, a single tear rolled down Bernice's cheek. She convinced herself that her eyes were red from the onions she was chopping for the Campbell family's dinner.

Flickering flames from the fireplace warmed the room, as the Campbells gathered around the fire. All the couples were hugged up, including David and April. It felt good to wrap his arms around someone as caring as April.

Bernice joined with the family in the peaceful warmth of the living room. All of the children were upstairs watching movies or playing on their tablets with stomachs full from the delectable gumbo, which was ready when they returned. David had taken them on a tour downtown. He succeeded in tiring them out, so he could spend quiet time with April.

A sense of tranquility blanketed the room, as the family laughed about their day and discussed plans for the rest of the holiday weekend. Chris jokingly prodded April about her life, because this was an opportunity for the family to get to know her. She spoke about her work and her own divorce experience, when Bernice asked if she'd ever been married.

As she spoke in calm, easy tones, family could relate to what she revealed. It was no wonder David and April hit it off so quickly. They spent the evening laughing and joking. April fit right in; it was as if she'd been a part of the family all along.

It was getting late and everyone decided to turn in for the night. April was reluctant to leave, because she enjoyed being with David and his family.

As the new couple walked out to April's car hand in hand, David turned to face her and gently grasped both her hands with his own. The two stood looking at each other smiling.

"I don't know what's going on, but I like it," David acknowledged. He prayed what he said made sense to her, as he spoke about his feelings for her. Looking into April's eyes, strong emotions almost overwhelmed him.

She smiled and agreed that she also enjoyed getting to know him.

After her declaration, David put his arms around her waist. April gently placed her hands on his shoulders. A hint of April's rose perfume scent permeated David's senses, as the two kissed for the first time. April gently caressed the back of David's neck. Her eyes flickered open, as the two quietly savored the moment. "Wow," she sighed softly.

David chuckled, "that was lovely," as he ran his hand down the left side of her cheek. "Will I see you tomorrow," he asked?

April exhaled quietly, nodding her head.

David smiled. "How about I come to you," he responded to her nonverbal agreement? "We'll spend the day together."

"What about your family," April inquired?

"Well, you know," everybody is doing something different tomorrow. It'll give us time to be alone."

She whispered ok, and David gave her a peck on the cheek before opening her car door. He waited until she was seated comfortably inside before closing it.

April started the car and waved goodbye, as she pulled into the quiet suburban street. He watched, until she turned the corner. When he turned to go back into the house, David noticed Bernice watching from the upstairs bedroom window. He could tell by the mean look on her face that she was not happy, but he didn't care. His ex-mother-in-law approval is not needed.

Chapter 15

Peeking out the window at the morning sunrise, David noted the vibrant color spectrum on the horizon. Light danced across the sky, reflecting his mood. He could barely contain his excitement about the day. He was spending it with April without anyone else around.

Since she loved sea animals and had never been to an aquarium, it was the perfect place for the two of them to spend time together. He'd ask her to choose what she wanted for dinner and end the day with a movie. April lived in Norcross, which is about 15 minutes from his home. She had driven to his house yesterday. He'd drive today. One thing is certain, he didn't want to be in her home alone. Sparks were already flying between them, and he didn't want to leave any room to temptation.

Arriving at her apartment around mid-afternoon, David smiled when April emerged looking stunning. They embraced, each reaching for the other's hand. He led her to the passenger side seat. After ensuring she was comfortably seated, he closed the door and walked around the front of the vehicle to the driver's side.

She smiled at him, as he hopped in, "so, what are we doing today?"

He grinned, as he contemplated his response. "It's a secret," David replied, winking at her.

"A secret," April laughed. "Well, this is exciting."

With one hand on the wheel, David gently grasped April's other hand, as he drove south on I85 and merged into traffic toward downtown Atlanta. They continued on the highway and exited on Williams St. As he drove, he anticipated what the day would be like. So far, he had not received any opposition from April.

In the past, Jackie always tried to pry information out of him with a bad attitude. He decided his ex-wife was just hard to please, and forced his thoughts away from Jackie to focus on his new girlfriend.

April was different, and he was different, determined this time around to let the lady choose, discuss, and collaborate.

There was a line of cars waiting to enter the parking garage. By now, Jackie would have been complaining, because they would have to wait to exit the vehicle. However, April's face lit up with delight, and she was indeed surprised.

"You're taking me to the aquarium," she smiled, as gratitude swelled up inside her. David grinned at her enthusiasm, because he hadn't seen a smile on a woman's face while on a date in a long time.

He reciprocated her smile with a big cheesy grin of his own. "You told me you love sea animals," David responded. "Why didn't you become a marine biologist?"

They both laughed at the question, because she knew that he meant it as a joke. David loved that she was in tune with his dry wit and sense of humor.

The couple spent hours viewing the sea animals, watching dolphins jump into the air and whales swim through the water. Both were amazed at the aquatic life. The two walked slowly through the aquarium hand in hand while sharing stories of their lives, enjoying time with each other.

April and David were getting hungry. A fleeting thought ran through his mind that his last dinner date was the night Tony was run down by a hit and run driver, who the police never found. He pushed those thoughts from the past away and stuck to his decision to let April choose the restaurant. To his surprise, she chose to eat at the aquarium.

The day was progressing better than he expected. April was funny, complemental, very appreciative and a joy to be around. She ordered just a burger and drink of water. David told her she could have whatever she wanted, no matter the cost. She chose one item, he wanted her to eat to her heart's content. April assured him that the burger was enough, so he also ordered a burger.

After they finished eating, the two sat at the table talking. April began to tell him about the trouble she's still having with her former best friend. It's been two years since she stole Robbie, but Leslie was still causing problems for her. April didn't know why she was acting out. Leslie had already gotten the man, there was no need for her to keep rubbing it in.

David told her about the time he had with Jackie, explaining to April that his ex-didn't appreciate the things he had done for her and her mother over the years. Every time he thought the relationship was heading in the right direction, another challenge popped up. For so long, the marriage was on a downward spiral, but he never wanted to admit it. The last thing in the world he wanted was a failed marriage.

Checking his watch, David noted they had about 30 minutes before the movie began. He still hadn't told April where they were going next, and it didn't bother her either. For that, David was grateful. He finally was able to surprise someone without any backlash.

After leaving the aquarium, the couple rode back north to the movie theater on Medlock Bridge. April's smile was as big as her first smile, when she realized he was taking her to the aquarium. David could see the delight in her eyes. She was enjoying herself.

The movie was the latest Star Wars and it was just as exciting as the previous movie in the saga. They talked about it all the way back to April's place. It was getting late, and neither wanted the night to end.

David walked April to her door. They stood facing each other holding hands. He wanted to speak, but he was kind of sheepish. "I," ...he paused not wanting to be disrespectful or inconsiderate. "I know we've spent the last two days together, and I know..."

April cut in. "I'd love to go to church with you and your family," she laughed, when she saw the relief and delight on his face.

David chuckled a little bit. "Thank you, I didn't know how to ask you."

"It's ok," she smiled. "I tell you what; why don't I cook dinner for all of you," April offered.

"Oh, I couldn't ask you to do that," he replied.

"No, I want to." She playfully batted her eyes at him.

He leaned back and laughed. "Alright, if you insist."

"Thank you."

"You're welcome."

David pulled April closer to him. His hands were around her waist and she encircled her arms around his neck. They both looked passionately at each other. He wanted to kiss her romantically but felt it would lead to other things. David gently touched her forehead with his lips. "Christian education starts at 8:30, pick you up at 8," he inquired?

April nodded her head. "I'll be ready." She wanted him to kiss her, but he pulled away.

David saw her house key in her hand, and he gently removed the key to open the door. He peeked inside to make sure the coast was clear. The door was narrow, so he stepped away to let April inside.

She walked in just a little bit then turned toward David. "I really enjoyed myself today," she spoke softly. "Thank you for a wonderful time."

David stood in the breezeway with his hands in his pockets. She had no idea how good that made him feel. "It was my pleasure," he responded, as a smile crept across his face and he burst with joy on the inside.

They both gave each other a nod and a smile, before April closed and locked the door.

In the present…

Michigan

Charles came to pick up Ashley and Tony last night, after Damon left. Jackie was grateful to her father, because she was scheduled to work double shifts at her new nursing position. She'd kept the news about passing the licensure exam to herself. For the first time in more than a decade, she'll earn money from her nursing career. In her new position, she was helping people, and she could make a good salary from working four 12-hour shifts per week.

She took the familiar trek to the hospital, where Tony recovered from his injuries. After parking, Jackie stepped out of the sedan to head toward the main entrance. Wearing blue nursing scrubs, she walked through the door with a smile on her face. Feeling great satisfaction and a sense of purpose, she actually liked herself for the first time in a long time.

Her floor's shift supervisor gave her the patient assignments. She logged into the software system to review the notes for her first patient. Walking confidently toward room J112, she knocked on the closed door and entered the room.

"Hello, Mr. Leonard," she said, smiling as she moved toward the patient to check his vitals. "How are you today?"

Jackie listened to her patient, as she gave him the doctor's prescription for codeine to help with his pain. After checking his vitals and noting his chart, she left the room. In her wake, she left air of empathy, which made Mr. Leonard feel better.

Every patient Jackie met that day pulled something different out of her. From encouraging quotes to quick-witted humor, Jackie's personality gave the patients hope. For herself, the work reminded her of why she became a nurse in the first place. Even when she came across a patient who was dealing with extreme health challenges, her attitude remained encouraging. Jackie quickly returning to the nurse's station to request assistance when necessary.

On her break, she thought about the text message she'd received from her mother. It was no wonder her mother went to David's for Christmas. She was trying to get him back for her. She did miss the lavish lifestyle. For sure, adjusting to living in the world without David was challenging. He always made sure she had everything she wanted, but her heart wasn't with him. For years, she'd wanted his brother Damon.

If David was seeing April, he had moved on. Jackie wanted to feel happy for him but couldn't stop the jealous emotions, which began to take hold of her. Damon couldn't offer her financial stability. As the day after Christmas continued, she realized that she made the wrong choice. Moving from patient to patient, Jackie was careful not to allow all the emotions she felt interfere with her interactions. She attempted to compartmentalize her thoughts, while she worked.

After being cared for so well for that long, she wanted it back. If she had been honest with David from the beginning, perhaps they could have worked through their problems. Possessive feelings swamped her, as she affirmed the truth to herself. *'David is my husband,'* she told herself. For the first time, she felt sorry for him. As feelings welled up within her, she knew she was feeling the deep pain and emotional turmoil, which he'd felt when he found out about Damon. David deserved better than her, she mused quietly. He needed someone who would reciprocate his feelings. 'I must be a better wife,' her thoughts ran through her mind, even as she returned to Mr. Leonard's room to check on him.

It was not easy to return to work, but her children were worth it. Most of her family and friends saw her as a spoiled brat with a princess syndrome. Even her own parents didn't believe in her. She had a different vision for herself. As she successfully performed her nursing duties, she realized that part of what had been missing in her relationship with David was her own sense of self-worth. She enjoyed working as a house wife and mother but also wanted a career.

She was glad that she and Damon were not living together. Her parents and Damon's parents were old fashioned and believed that a man and woman should not cohabitate, unless they're family or married. The Campbell's view was more of a spiritual stand. Jackie's parents were just stuck in thinking from their generation. Both sets of parents threatened to cut off financial help, if they moved in together. It was disappointing. Damon made enough money to care for himself mainly. There was barely enough for him to give to her for the children. Now that she was going to have the money to support herself, she knew that she and Damon should definitely not live together. Especially since, he refused to get a second job or search for a better paying job. Damon's lack of drive angered Jackie.

Her lawyer told her that she should have waited until after the divorce decree to remove David's name from the birth certificates. It would have put her in a better position to ask him for money. Besides David's job, there was the real estate, laundry mat, and a car wash. All of these channels brought in more than enough finances.

Over the years David showed her how to budget and manage money. They had no debt, credit cards, car loans, or student loans, and the house was even paid off. He stopped paying the car insurance and gave her a car repair and replacement fund. She realized that David gave her more than money. He took care of them in other ways, ensuring he planned out all the details of their lives.

She decided to send Damon a text message to remind him to pick up the children from her father's house after work.

Across town, Damon's phone buzzed with the message. He thought about the secret he needed to share with Jackie, but really didn't know how she'd respond. Jackie wanted him to pick up the kids from grandfather Charles' home. He planned to introduce Tony and Ashley to their brother, Dominique and finally let Jackie know about this part of his life.

Damon was at his workstation. He thought about his family in Atlanta and wondered what they were doing. Anger rose within him because they all left him behind. He wasn't invited, and didn't blame his brother. In truth, he didn't see how David did it. His brother took care of five children, a princess wife, his parents, and his mother-in-law.

Damon wiped his arm across his forehead. It was hot near the manufacturer's oven but freezing outside. His mind drifted to the argument he had with Jackie. She was complaining that he wasn't helping out like he should. That's been her cry, ever since she and David split up. He was tired of hearing it.

Damon missed his old life and the freedom to come and go as he pleased. He loved Jackie, but she was too needy. That aspect about her was unknown to him. David never mentioned it, and Damon never saw her needy behavior until now.

Damon recalled Jackie's blow-up last night. The argument was one of the worst they'd had. The relationship was overwhelming with the added responsibility of raising Ashley, Tony and Dana. Damon smirked, because he felt even more respect and gratitude for his parents. They made many sacrifices for the family throughout the years. Raising children was a big responsibility, and now he had four youngsters who depended on him.

He felt that Jackie needed to cut the strings some, and loosen her hold on him. Damon couldn't hang out with his friends. She never understood a guy's night out. Guys night out meant no women and definitely no children. Every time he wanted to go somewhere by himself, they argued.

It didn't matter that the two of them had their own places. As soon as she got off work, she was calling him. Either she wanted to stop by or he had to come to her. Damon didn't have a moment of peace, except at work or at Bridget's house. All these thoughts ran through Damon's mind.

He thought about his life and started scolding himself again for not obtaining a college degree like his siblings, but he wasn't interested.

Life was different now. His job didn't pay much, and he has a lot of mouths to feed. Jackie and the children were depending on him. Most of the time he just wanted to cut out and run from it all. At those times, he'd remember Tony's deep, reflective eyes, Dana's fiery, honest disposition, and Ashley's sad emotional state. These were his children, and he had to give them as much love as possible.

He sighed, as he thought about the relationships with his family and friends. His closest friends stopped talking to him because of what he did to his brother. They all sided with David, discouraging him from pursuing a relationship with Jackie. The relationship with his family wasn't any better. David had been the only one that allowed him to come and go, as he pleased. Micki never allowed him in her home, unless the family was gathering for an event. She definitely didn't want him there now. Chris only allowed him to come if he made plans beforehand, and he couldn't stay long.

At lunchtime, Damon spoke with Aunt Gladys and learned that David was moving on with his life. Aunt Gladys was the only family member he could confide in. Damon spoke of how he missed his brother David and all the times they'd spent together.

As twins, the two got along well, rarely arguing and sharing just about everything. Unfortunately, Damon took it too far by sharing David's wife. He thought David would come around by now, but his brother kept avoiding him. Damon reached out to his brother daily, apologizing via voicemail or text. Each time, he hoped David would respond, but it never happened.

He told Aunt Gladys that he wished he could have done things differently and asked her repeatedly what he could do to mend the broken relationship with his twin brother.

She said that he must break off the relationship he has with Jackie, and give David time to heal. Aunt Gladys felt that their relationship may never get back to where it was, but they would speak again.

The horn blew to let the workers know that the work day had come to an end. Damon was caught in his thoughts, and didn't hear it blow. A coworker got his attention. He was still loading parts into the oven.

"Hey man, it's time to go," Damon's coworker informed him. "What are you hoping for overtime or something?"

He stared at his coworker and laughed. "No, I'm not looking for overtime, I didn't hear the whistle blow." Damon started cleaning his area and waited for the last part to finish heating.

He didn't know how he was going to support Jackie and the children. His salary was significantly smaller than David's income. David had income property and businesses on the side, as well as his job. Damon was nowhere near earning that much money. He knew Jackie and the children missed the lifestyle that they once enjoyed. Dana was taking it the hardest. She looked forward to daddy-daughter nights with David and going out to eat.

Damon sat in his vehicle at the parking lot of the factory. *'I just have to do something to make more money',* he thought to himself, with his head in his hands. *'I've got to heal these relationships that I've broken.'* He reached in his glove compartment to take out the little pocket Bible that Bridget put in his car. Flipping through the pages, he found the scripture he was seeking.

"The *Lord* is my shepherd," Damon said quietly, as he focused on the words in the tiny book in his hands. "I shall not want..." A phone call from Bridget caused his phone to vibrate, just as he finished the prayer.

Bridget's father had made some renovations to a building he owned. He'd purchased it for Bridget's mother, so she could start her own restaurant. Bridget convinced her father to let Damon use the facility instead, if he gave her dad a portion of the proceeds. He'd only mentioned to Bridget once a long time ago that he'd thought of opening a restaurant.

"Wow," Damon said to himself after he hung up the phone. "You are right on time, *Lord.*" He didn't think he'd all of a sudden become super religious. However, after the miraculously answered prayer, he'd make sure to pray more often.

Damon started the car to go pick up Tony and Ashley. After the Campbell's returned from Atlanta, Damon planned to enlist the help of his mother and Bridget to raise money for his pop-up restaurant. He even started the menu in his mind, including ribs, barbeque chicken, fried chicken, catfish, and a choice of sides. Damon was a good cook. He always shared his four-cheese macaroni and cheese at family events. With Aunt Gladys' pound cake recipe, the restaurant was sure to succeed.

Chapter 16

A week later, Deloris and Bridget agreed to help Damon cook and serve food, so he began advertising. He distributed flyers everywhere near the restaurant. Damon solicited coworkers, friends, and family. His parents informed their church family and their friends. Bridget let her family and friends know as well.

He wanted to involve his children, but didn't want Jackie to know. Her hands would be stretched out for more money. In the meantime, he would give what he could to help her.

Bridget thought that if the sales were good, they should consider getting a booth at the Trade Center, which opened on the weekends to aspiring restaurants and other businesses. He pondered on it for a while. It would be a good way for both of them to make extra money.

Damon was thrilled Joseph and Chris agreed to help with the grilling. All it took was for him to put forth an effort to better himself, and his parents and brother were right there to support him. He now wanted the life his siblings and parents enjoyed. Everyone was well off financially except him. That was about to change. Bridget made him realize how much more he could do with his life.

The restaurant opened at 11 a.m. Family and friends were there working together. Much to his surprise, Micki walked in with carryout plates, napkins, and plastic ware. A bunch of Micki's friends placed orders. Micki wanted to help deliver orders at no charge. Damon hugged his sister in gratitude. For the first time, his proactive plans gave his family hope that he wanted to change.

Bridget and Deloris worked well in the kitchen together, collaborating to get the orders out. Micki's orders were filled first, since no one else had arrived yet. She went to deliver them to her best friend's hair salon. When she came back, she had ten more orders from her customers.

The two cooks handled the bustling kitchen like pros, while Damon, Chris, and Joseph stayed busy on the grill. Deloris filled the next set of Micki's orders, while Bridget took care of those who entered the restaurant. By 6 p.m. everything was sold out, and they had served everyone.

After setting aside the money for Bridget's father, Damon walked away with $1500. He offered to give his helpers compensation, but they all refused.

After they cleaned up the restaurant, everyone agreed to meet at Joseph's and Deloris' home. Damon wanted to speak to his family and just fellowship. He missed out on the Thanksgiving and Christmas gatherings. After returning from Atlanta, the family shared with him everything they had experienced. When Damon heard that David was seeing April, he knew his brother was moving forward with his life.

Damon arrived at his parents' home; everyone was already there. The family came straight over after the dinner sale. Bridget went home to pick up Dominique. He'd told his mother that he had something to tell the family. Not one to beat around the bush, Deloris got straight to the point. "So, what did you want to talk to us about," she asked bluntly?

Damon raised one eyebrow, shook his head, and then smiled. "Alright everyone, I have someone I'd like you to meet," he exclaimed with excitement. Moving quickly toward the front entrance, Damon waited patiently for Dominique and Bridget. When they stepped on the porch, Damon opened the door. He could see the look of confusion on everyone's face. Bridget stepped inside, holding a little bundle, which was wrapped from head to toe in a blue baby blanket.

The family looked puzzled. Joseph's eyebrows came together. Deloris jerked her head back. Joseph looked at Damon, and he could see them questioning him with their eyes. Micki had a smirk on her face. Chris just shook his head.

Damon gave everyone a smile, as he gently guided Bridget to the sofa. "Family, you already know Bridget, and this here is my son Dominique," he explained.

Deloris was the first to speak. "Did you say your son," she asked with joy? She made her way over to Bridget to hug and kiss her.

"Yes ma'am, I did," he replied, giving his family a big smile, as he watched their expressions evolve from confusion to joy.

"Bridget is this your son," Deloris asked, as she sat next to Bridget to get a peek at her new grandson?

"Yes, he is," Bridget replied proudly.

Dominique reached out his little arms to hug his grandmother, as she drew near to them. She gladly wrapped her arms around him.

"Well come here boy, and give your grandpa a hug," Joseph said, also moving toward Dominique. Deloris let the child go briefly, so that Joseph could hold him.

Damon could see the look of joy on his mother's face was mixed with worry. "I am so happy to have Dominique and Bridget," he told his family, hoping to convince himself and his family that he was ready to handle the responsibility.

"Bridget, if you don't mind, I'd like to keep him one weekend to get to know him better," Deloris offered. She believed that she should know each one of her grandchildren personally.

"I'd like that," Bridget responded joyfully. "I'm sure he would like it as much." Bridget reached out and gave Deloris a hug.

"Would you like that, buddy," Damon asked his son in a baby voice?

Everyone broke out into laughter, when Dominique moved his head up and down, as if he understood.

Deloris wanted the rest of the family to meet Dominique so she invited them back for Sunday dinner. Her eyebrows came together, as if deep in thought, before asking about the elephant in the room.

"What about Jackie," Deloris inquired? "Does she know about Dominique?"

Damon took a deep breath. "I am going to tell her soon," he replied.

"Oh, if I could be a fly on the wall for that conversation," Micki interjected.

"Micki, not in front of Bridget and the child," Deloris cautioned her daughter, because she didn't want Dominique to hear about any drama. She believed babies were tiny recorders, taking note of every word and action.

"A fly on the wall," Micki repeated, ignoring her mother and quietly laughing to herself at the thought of Jackie finding out.

In the present...

Georgia

David planned a date out with April Saturday night. They both enjoyed jazz music so he decided to take her to a jazz restaurant and lounge in Atlanta on Marietta Street.

Aunt Gladys volunteered to watch of the twins. According to Georgia law, they were too young to stay home by themselves. Both of them protested to having a babysitter. He didn't tell them who it was, so that he could surprise them. Aunt Gladys would keep them laughing all night. She always had funny stories to tell, and it was always a joy to be in her company.

David dressed in a black suit, white shirt, and a red tie. He asked April to dress in her best attire. The air was chilly but not too cold. The lounge opens at 9 p.m. He wanted to be there when the doors opened.

When eight o'clock rolled around, he headed out to get April. Aunt Gladys arrived at 7:30. The twins were ecstatic because Gladys kept everyone in stitches with laughter. His black SUV was sparkling on the outside, the car had been detailed earlier that day. It looked brand new. He pulled up to April's building, there was nowhere to park so he pulled behind the two parked cars closest to the walkway.

David knocked on the door. When April opened the door, she smiled. He was amazed at her beauty.

"Wow!"

April gave him a big smile. "Was that for me," she asked teasingly.

"Yes, it was and you look great," he responded! David held out his arm, and April took hold of it.

After she locked her door, they headed to the car. David, always the gentleman, opened the door for April. When she was seated, he walked around to the driver side and jumped in.

"You look great too, my handsome one," she said. "So, where are we headed?"

"It's a surprise," he said, winking at her. David always like to keep people in a state of anticipation.

"You're spoiling me with all these surprises, you know." She said teasingly, but she enjoyed every bit of his surprises.

They arrived at the jazz lounge, and David pulled up to the valet. As April noticed the name of the lounge, her face lit up like a Christmas tree.

"I've always wanted to come here," her voice's excitement pleased David.

"Why haven't you," he asked?

"I didn't have anyone to go with," she replied. Her ex-husband didn't have an interest in jazz, so he was against it when she suggested it for a date night.

David chuckled. As they entered the lounge, a jazz artist was on stage. Perfect rhythmic beats floated through the air. The lights in the lounge were dim. There was a mixture of round and square tables. At the entrance door, there was a counter for coat check in and a cash register to pay for entry. Straight ahead of the couple, a wide three step staircase led to the lounge area.

The couple sat as close to the stage as possible. There was a bar on the left side. Neither one of them drank, so they ordered pop until they were ready to eat.

Each of the artists that appeared sang or played hit jazz songs, some current and others were older. The music was enjoyable, and David and April sat side by side relishing in the other's presence.

April was getting hungry, so they ordered barbecue chicken wings and fries. It wasn't an elegant meal, but it was something they both enjoyed. Even though he could have afforded the expensive meal, he was pleased she chose something economical. David purposely set aside money to cover his dates with April, whatever they didn't use was just left in the pot for another time. He didn't adjust the budget to account for the money not spent. In case she wanted to have an elegant night out, he would be ready.

As the night progressed, each jazz musician showcased their talent, playing complex musical combinations and awe-inspiring solo performances. Every one of them performed with soulful expression and the crowd cheered each artist's performance.

It was getting late and they headed out. David hated to see the date night end, but they were meeting again for church in the morning. He couldn't wait.

On the way home, April kept thanking David and telling him how much she enjoyed the evening. Her comments made David happy, he had never received such compliments. Suddenly there was a pause, David couldn't make out why she stopped talking.

"Are you ok," he asked?

She took a deep breath. "I know we ate at the lounge, but I'm craving a muffin right now."

David raised his eyebrows. "Oh, so you like muffins," he responded.

"I love muffins; blueberry is my favorite."

David drove to a donut shop, which was opened 24 hours to purchase muffins for April. At the moment, he decided that would be his nickname for her, Muffin.

He pulled up to her apartment and parked. The pair sat in the car to converse for a while. April was telling David about a possible job promotion. He heard every word she said, but his mind was also focused on how well they were getting along.

April noticed David's mind was elsewhere, so she faked a yawn.

David jumped out of his seat and ran to April's door. He flung it opened as if he was trying to rescue her from a fire.

April was startled, she'd never seen him run so fast. "Is something wrong," she said with a look of confusion on her face?

"No, you're tired, and I'm keeping you from getting some rest." David reached out his hand for April to grab hold as she stepped out of the SUV.

"You heard me yawn, but you didn't hear anything else I said." A disappointed look shrouded her face. David could also hear it in her voice

"I did hear everything," he assured her. As they stood facing each other, David repeated the words she had spoken. While he was talking, her demeanor changed from disappointment to delight.

"I'm sorry, I thought your mind was somewhere else," she said "I kind of got an attitude, so I pretended to yawn." She poked out her bottom lip in a playful way.

David pulled her into a hug. "That's ok, let's get you inside." He pulled back and kissed her on the cheek.

April looped her arm around David's as they walked to her door. "What are we going to do tomorrow?"

David thought about that for a minute. "How about the twins and I spend the day with you here at your place."

April smiled, shrugged her left shoulder and bent her head down as if she was posing for a picture. "I'd like that, I'll whip up something for dinner."

"Ok, I look forward to it."

April wrapped her arms around David's neck. He held on to her waist. They stood that way for a while; April could tell he was pondering over something. "Do you want to talk about it?"

He smiled at her. "One day, but not right now."

As their lips met, passion ran through their bodies, and the kiss was getting hotter. When they separated, their eyes met and they wanted more affection. Both of them backed away, because neither was ready to take the relationship to the next level.

April turned to open her door. When she stepped inside, David peaked inside. "Does it look the same," he asked? He would've gone inside to make sure she was safe, but he thought it best to stay outside due to raging hormones.

April walked around her apartment, and everything was intact. She came back to the door and gave David a thumbs up. A thought crossed her mind to invite him in, but David closed her door shut. Deep down inside, she was grateful, all kinds of thoughts and emotions were running rampant. She silently thanked God for David having the strength to walk away, because she was thinking about how wonderful it would feel to hold him in bed.

The following Saturday, David noticed that the twins were sad. They'd enjoyed the family visit for the holidays. Unfortunately, their spirits were down, since everyone had returned home. He decided to cheer them up by doing everything they enjoyed, such as bowling, skating, and going to the movies.

They started the day with breakfast at a pancake house. The scrumptious smelling aroma of a variety of choice flap jacks wafted through the air. The twins heard their friends talk about the banana, strawberry, blueberry, and chocolate chip pancakes, expressing to David that they wanted to try it.

It was a cozy little place. When you enter the double doors, two long benches with green cushions flank each side of the wall in the waiting area. A red brick wall stood at the front end of the restaurant. The walkway was wide enough for others to walk through without bumping into anyone, even if both benches were full.

The restaurant was packed, since it was Saturday morning. The twins were hungry and couldn't wait to sink their teeth into the tasty breakfast cuisine. The three of them settled on the bench for the twenty-minute wait.

David watched as each person passed him, as they were exiting or entering. He noticed a lot of families were dining together this hot weekend morning. Most of the diners were composed of groups, each including an adult male and female. He reasoned that the couples were probably husbands and wives. A family of five exited, as he and the twins waited on the bench.

He thought about the times in the past when he would take his family out for breakfast. The children spent the whole time laughing and snatching food off each other's plates, while he and Jackie cracked jokes. He missed his family.

After breakfast, he took the twins to downtown Atlanta. The first stop was the World of Coca Cola. The family toured the soda company. Junior and Nakita got a kick out of the fountain. The fountain was circular and cola would shoot out. Cups were available at the fountain, so visitors could catch the drink as it shot out. The twins drank as much as their stomachs would allow.

The family learned how the company produces the cola. Viewing the factory through large glass windows, David and the twins watched the process with other tourists.

After the Coca Cola tour, David took the twins to a family fun center in the city. There they bowled, skated, played games, and snacked. He had his cousins meet him with their children. The twins were preteens and wanted to separate from the adults.

The family started out with bowling. David won the first games with more than 200 points. Mitchell, his older cousin, wanted a rematch. However, the children wanted to roller skate. After skating, the group decided to play skeet ball and other games. Laser tag was last on the list. Everyone enjoyed shooting each other with a laser gun. The children still had plenty of energy, so the parents let them keep playing.

David and his cousins ordered food, while catching up with one another. They reminisced about old times, how each mother would group her family together to travel for a visit. Taking turns, the Campbell's would travel to Georgia one year and then the Hicks came to Michigan the next year. They all enjoyed good times back in the day. Each cousin expressed what they remembered about those times. The day passed quickly, and soon it was late afternoon.

He spent the afternoon surfing Facebook and talking with the family back home for a few hours. In the quietness of his home, David's mind drifted back to Jackie and the children. It isn't fair to have their lives change so drastically, but what choice did he have? Jackie would never go for all of them relocating to Georgia.

The whole purpose of leaving Michigan was to get a fresh start and not see Jackie and Damon together. In the evening, after checking with April, he loaded the twins into his vehicle to head to her home for dinner.

In the present...

Michigan

Damon felt relief when the horn rang, signaling an end to the night shift. It was time to reveal his secret to Jackie and her family. He had to make a couple of stops first. He didn't know how she'd take the news, but he had to tell her. All kinds of thoughts ran through his mind. What would her parents say? How will the children react? Most importantly, what would Jackie say? Their relationship was rocky. Ever since she parted ways from David, he wasn't even as attracted to her as much as before.

As he pulled into the driveway, nervousness covered him like a swarm of bees on a bed of roses. Perspiration ran down his face, and his racing heart beat wildly within him. There was no reason for him to be nervous, but he hated rejection. His family rejected him, once his betrayal was revealed. Even though his relationship with the family was better since he started selling dinners.

He prepared his mind, because there was no way to change the past. Ironically, David's words from the past kept him going. He remembered his twin telling him years ago to face his fears, even when it was difficult. As he remembered, David's voice ran through his mind, *'don't let fear stop you from accomplishing your ambitions; conquer it and you will be able to stop fear dead in its tracks.'* It was his brother's encouragement, which helped him to overcome challenges from the past. He would not let this situation stop him either.

It was cold outside, and a light layer of snow blanketed the ground. The living room light was on, and he could see some of the bedroom lights on upstairs. Jackie's home looked quiet from where he sat inside the warmth of his vehicle.

Damon stopped stalling and opened the door to step outside into the cold. He walked around to the passenger door to unstrap Dominique's car seat. He pressed the vehicle's remote key button, hearing the familiar beeping noise. He didn't want to fight tonight. Jackie made it clear that she didn't want him spending time with anyone else but her and their children. She didn't say it verbatim, but her disapproval of him leaving on Christmas evening to visit with others led him to that conclusion. Today, she'd have to understand that he couldn't give her all of his time.

As Damon knocked on the door, his hands were still sweating. After the second knock, he wiped one hand on his pants and held the car seat with his other hand. Jackie opened the door grinning ear to ear. Her face always lit up when he came around, even when she was married to David. She opened the door for him to come in. As he stepped inside the doorway, he was watching her facial expression. Jackie's smile quickly turned into a frown.

Damon swiftly walked into the kitchen.

Jackie was on his heels. "What's this," she asked him haughtily?

"Can you call the children down," he asked, giving her a sheepish look.

She stood with her hands on her hips staring at him.

"Please," Damon pleaded.

After a brief pause, she walked to the stairs and called them down.

The three came running down the stairs, as they rounded the corner, the children were surprised at what they saw.

Damon took a deep breath. "I'd like for you all to meet Dominique, my son and your brother," he offered, as he gently removed Dominique from the car seat and began to remove his coat. There, he'd finally done it. Damon mentally pat himself on the back and encouraged himself silently, even as he noted Jackie's wide-eyed expression of complete surprise.

"Our brother," Tony exclaimed in excitement!

"He's your what," Jackie prodded, still standing with her hands on her hips and her mouth gaped opened?

"He's my son," Damon confirmed, standing with his eight-month-old son Dominique in his arms. He was light skinned with curly hair and looked a lot like Damon.

Jackie stared at the baby harshly. Damon asked the children to go upstairs for a moment, so that he and Jackie could talk privately.

As soon as the children were out of ear shot, Jackie started in on Damon. "I can't believe this," she said. "You had a child with another woman?"

"Are you serious right now," Damon replied? "We are not going to argue in front of my son."

"How old is this boy," Jackie asked, as a bout of jealousy overcame her.

"He's eight months," Damon replied.

"Eight months," she exclaimed! You do realize that you conceived him during the time we were serious with each other."

"And, you do realize that you were married to my brother for 15 years." His tone was sharp. Even though he knew Jackie wouldn't approve, it still was disappointing.

Jackie turned her back to Damon and his son. "You never told me you were sleeping with someone else." A sob caught in her throat. "Why are you bringing him here now?"

"Because, I can no longer hide him," he explained. My family met him, and I figured you would find out soon anyway." Truth be told, he was shocked that she didn't know about Dominique already.

Jackie sucked her teeth and spewed out the words. "This isn't fair Damon!" She spoke louder than she expected, but it was how she felt.

"What's not fair," he asked in confusion?

"It was just supposed to be us and our children, not some random woman's child," Jackie retorted, as her mind reviewed the last year. Now everything was starting to make sense. Damon didn't have money for her and her children, because he was helping to support someone else.

"What do you mean," he asked her? "Are you saying that you can't love Dominique?"

She swung around to face him, tears streaming down her face. "That's exactly what I'm saying."

"Can't or won't," he asked?

"Both," Jackie replied defiantly.

The two stood there facing each other. Deep down inside this was a win for Damon. He and Jackie didn't see eye to eye on many things, and it caused a rift between them. If Jackie couldn't love his son, then she wasn't worth all of the drama that came with their relationship. "Well as disappointing as this is for you, I can't change the past. He's here and he's mine."

"That's why you wanted to leave early Christmas evening to be with them," Jackie questioned him? Jealousy permeated her spirit, as she all but forgot that she'd decided that she and Damon were not a good fit for each other.

"Yes, I left to spend time with my son," he exclaimed!

"You know who I'm talking about, Dominique and his mother." She flung her arms toward Damon, gesturing toward Dominique, who cooed softly from his arms.

"I brought him here, so you and the children could meet him," Damon explained in exasperation, as he stepped away from Jackie. He was fed up with the situation.

"Whoa," Jackie replied. "You've got to be joking."

"What is the problem, Jackie," Damon asked?

"You're not going to spend time with me, and you're just going to take the children and leave me here," she retorted.

"Why is that such a bad thing to spend time with my children without you," he implored?

"I don't have time for this," Damon replied. "I am not allowing Dominique to remain in a hostile situation. We're leaving, because you've made it perfectly clear you don't want Dominique around." Damon stormed upstairs to retrieve the children, marched them to the car, and strapped Domonique in the baby seat for the ride.

Jackie watched helplessly from the window. She knew that she had reacted poorly but could not help all the emotions welling up from deep within her. She thought about the 'love in action' words that her father shared with her. *'David would have prepared her in advance for an emotionally draining situation by having a conversation about it first,'* Jackie thought to herself. Still, she couldn't blame her emotional response on Damon's fly by the seat of your pants actions.

By the time Damon pulled into the mall, he'd forgotten all about Jackie's drama. He was enjoying his time with his children, and was so glad that he didn't have to keep any more secrets.

It was Bridget's sad look on Christmas evening and Jackie's pressure that led him to spill the beans. He couldn't have made a better decision. Dominique was having a ball with his family. Deloris already wanted him to spend a weekend with them, so they can get to know each other. He can see his parents now spoiling Dominique with all kinds of toys, gadgets, and clothes.

His biggest problem is Jackie. It's like she couldn't function without him around. Her neediness was a big turnoff. She never did that to David, because he wasn't what she wanted. He and David would spend hours together and Jackie would only call David once. In contrast, David sent Jackie text messages throughout the day. It wasn't until he and Jackie stopped hiding that he realized her obsession. She was possessive and a little controlling. Damon didn't want to be controlled; he wanted to feel free.

For so long, he wanted Jackie's physical body. The stolen moments that they spent together were not building blocks for a strong future, and David's shadow would forever hang between them. However, his relationship with Bridget was more mature and based in supporting one another in their walk with God. He never focused much on his spiritual life, but Bridget helped him to see life differently. He truly felt like he finally belonged to someone.

Tony broke Damon out of his reverie. "Can we go see a movie, Dad?"

Damon thought for a moment. A movie sounded good. He would let Tony pick the film. He started to tell them not to tell their mother, but he didn't care about what her response would be. She's been complaining that they never have enough money to do anything. If she started trippin' when he drops the them off, then he would simply leave.

"A movie it is," he replied with a hearty laugh.

The three jumped for joy, and Dominique smiled in Damon's arms. Damon used his phone to search for a children's movie. Tony chose a cartoon feature that he thought his baby brother would enjoy. Dana protested to no avail. She's a teen and dreaded watching cartoons. After the theater, Damon brought Dominique home first because the children needed to meet his mother, Bridget. Plus, he didn't want his son rebuffed by Jackie. The visit took longer than he expected. Bridget invited them in and fixed the three children hot chocolate. Surprisingly, they were reluctant to leave, enjoying Bridget's kind hospitality and friendly demeanor. Damon looked at his watch and ushered them out the door to return Ashley, Tony and Dana to Jackie.

Chapter 17

Jackie was frustrated. Damon hadn't been by so that she could speak with him. Days had gone by and there was no word from him. When she went to his apartment, his car wasn't there. She knocked on the door anyway, still there was no response. At times, she thought about going to his job, but she decided against it. It bothered her to call his parents to get a hold of him, but they couldn't get him to respond to her either. If it wasn't for him sending her child support, she would have already filed with the court.

Damon was supposed to pick up the children for the weekend, but he informed Dana that he would come next week. It nagged her that he would call their daughter and not call her. The more she thought about it, the more it seems that Damon had chosen to be with Dominique's mother. Even if they weren't going to be together, things had to be made right between them. She had no right yelling at him. She realized he introduced Dominique to her, so why wouldn't he introduce the other children to Dominique's mother. He still should have discussed it with her. Damon lacked basic communications skills. Jackie's mind focused on reconciliation, but how could she when he was clearly ignoring her. They hadn't really spoken since that night. When he wanted the children, he would send word through one of the three.

Fear and uncertainty overwhelmed her. Damon may be in a relationship with Dominique's mother. Jackie couldn't remember her name. Sorrow and despair crept in, before she knew it. She wanted more than ever to visit at his home again, but her car was down and she didn't feel comfortable leaving the children at home by themselves. Dana was a teenager, but the children argued more now than they ever did in the past. Even when they disagreed, David never left her feeling unsure about their relationship.

Jackie stood at the sliding door looking out at the backyard. Snow was still on the ground, even as spring was quickly approaching. She took a deep breath. Her mother's words started playing in her mind. *'He's going to pick up one day and leave you alone to take care of these kids,'* her mother told her. They were right here in the kitchen, when Bernice spoke those words in front of Damon. It was obvious her mother knew what kind of man he really was from her own experiences. Like her mother, Jackie chose poorly. Her mother left a good man. Now Jackie faced the same fate.

Jackie stood at the sliding door crying uncontrollably. *Why she couldn't love David, who had loved her so much all those years,* she questioned herself silently? The man she chose hadn't really chosen her. She realized that Damon never really loved her at all. Suddenly, Jackie realized that she may remain alone like her mother and raise children by herself. She had to do something to get David back and decided a trip to Atlanta is needed. Dana came into the room to show her a text message that she'd just received from Damon. He wanted to pick her and Ashley up from school the next day.

Damon laughed to himself as he thought about the sneaky way that was done to grab Dana and Ashley's DNA, while staring out the window. As the days went by, he felt like looking at the girls' test results. Bridget had the results in her possession. She had only asked him to review them a couple of times. Each time, he wasn't ready. She didn't push the issue, and Damon was grateful for her patience. However, something kept nagging at him to review the tests. Spring break was approaching, and Jackie had mentioned in a text that she wanted him to take the children for the week.

He and Bridget had a system going. Both worked a day job and an evening job. Bridget had a more flexible schedule, so she would stay home with their son most nights. Deloris, Joseph, Chris, and Micki also helped with Dominique. Bridget often worked when Damon was off. Taking care of four children every day would strain his time and drain his income.

He was on his lunch break, as he thought about what he needed to do. Once he reviewed the results, then he would go see Jackie.

Bridget was aware of his decision to speak with her. If she was available, he'd go visit her when his shift was over.

Looking down at the ham sandwich on honey wheat bread with lettuce, American cheese, and tomatoes, he realized how grateful he was for Bridget and all the little things she did to make his life easier. Unfortunately, he didn't feel much like eating. Thoughts of the paternity tests were at the forefront of his mind. He couldn't put off reviewing the test results any longer. Damon sent Bridget a text message informing her that he would be over after work.

Their relationship appeared to be getting better. He's hinted a couple of times that he was interested in having a long-lasting relationship with her. Either she was not taking him seriously or something else was going on. Bridget avoided the subject altogether.

His thoughts went to his brother David, whose marriage he'd busted up. Now he didn't even want Jackie, whom he'd coveted for so many years. David loved Jackie with all his heart. All along, Damon knew what he was doing was wrong on all levels. At first, he worried that his brother would find out. After a while, it didn't bother him. Jackie and Damon thought they were careful most of the time. It never dawned on him that any of those children were his. Now he's responsible for three of them, at least until he looks at the paternity results. After work, he sent Bridget a text message that he was on his way.

Bridget busied herself cleaning the house and waiting for Damon. He was finally ready to see the paternity tests. He gave the results to her to hold, but she hadn't opened the envelope. She decided to wait, until Damon was ready. They weren't actually a couple, even though Damon spent time at her home, as if they were together romantically. However, Bridget knew that he was still entangled with Jackie. She didn't want to get too emotionally attached, until he showed her that he was ready to commit to her fully.

She shook her head, as she thought of how Damon betrayed his own brother. Bridget told him that he had to fix his family relationships. Since he broke his brother's heart, it was his responsibility to make things right. Damon arrived at Bridget's house quicker than she thought he would. "Did you fly here," she teased? "How in the world did you get here so fast?"

He smiled, as she spoke. Her smile brightened his day. At that moment, he thought of how lovely it would be to wake up to her beautiful face every day.

Bridget tilted her head, looking at him curiously. "Why are you staring at me," she asked?

Damon was caught off guard by her question. "Oh, I was just admiring how pretty you are," he replied, a sheepish grin spreading across his face.

The sweet compliment warmed her heart. "Well, thank you, Damon," she replied. "But you didn't come here to sweet talk me." She walked over to her entertainment center to retrieve the test results from a drawer. She handed the envelope to Damon before sitting down on the couch.

Bridget's mood changed from playful to serious in an instant. Damon didn't know what to make of it. At times, Bridget seemed guarded. It was true; he was not there to talk sweet to her, but to find out if he is Ashley and Dana's father.

Bridget held the manila envelope in her hand. Damon's heart was racing. Secretly, he hoped only Tony belonged to him, but he had a feeling that wouldn't be the case.

As he started to open the envelope, his body began to perspire. After he pulled the papers out, he slowly read the results to Bridget. There was no emotion on her face, as she listened to Damon. He handed her the papers, so that she could read them for herself. Dana was not his daughter.

Damon took the papers out of Bridget's hands. The whole time he watched her for any sign, which indicated how she felt about the matter. She gave no hint, not even a sigh of relief. He stood with the papers in his hands, and eyes cast to the floor.

Bridget stood there watching. He waited for her response. She gave none, and the silence in the room engulfed them. After a minute or two, Bridget stood up to give him a comforting hug. He knew that she understood his emotions. He was both relieved and sad that Dana was not his child.

As the two of them stood looking at each other, Bridget spoke first. "What is your plan," she inquired? Compassion was in her voice. Her heart went out to him, because she knew that he was experiencing a loss.

Damon didn't know what to make of it. Jackie swore up and down that she'd only been with him and David, but she must have lied. Who is the other father? How could she have slept with someone other than the two of them?

All kinds of thoughts ran through his mind, and then it finally dawned on him. It didn't matter that Dana didn't belong to him, because he just didn't want to be with Jackie anymore. His decision rejuvenated in him. A smile spread across his face.

Bridget twisted her head, as her brows came together watching Damon's expression change. Damon seemed excited, instead of confused or angry. "Why are you smiling," she asked?

"Do you know what this means," he said, not waiting for her to answer. "I am free." He knew that being the father of only one of Jackie's children may help to heal the rift with David, but he's the father of two. More than anything, Damon wanted his brother back. As he explained his feelings to Bridget, he noted the intense expression on her face.

Bridget thought Damon was finally going to face his responsibilities, once he read the results. Disappointment washed over her, as he spoke about his plans to use the results to end his long-standing relationship with Jackie, instead of telling her the truth. Bridget thought Damon was mistaken to believe the results alone would mend the broken relationship with his brother. She responded to Damon with her honest opinions, causing him to reflect on the best way forward. Bridget was right. Damon decided to sit down with Jackie to talk about the results, their relationship, and the best way to co-parent Ashley and Tony.

After a frank discussion, the two decided that Damon should tell his parents Deloris and Joseph first. Giving Bridget a hug, Damon walked out of her apartment to drive to his parents' house. Sunlight warmed the passenger seat inside his car, but he barely noticed the heat. Carefully placing the test results on the seat beside him, Damon started the vehicle and rolled out of the parking lot into the flow of traffic.

Miles away, Deloris and Joseph were enjoying an evening together at home. They discussed what the family was planning for the upcoming holidays. David had already expressed that he would bring the twins home after school let out in late May. The children in Michigan would still be in school, but the twins missed the family back home and couldn't wait until mid-June. The couple wanted to have a family gathering, welcoming David back to his home state. He wasn't moving back, and he hadn't been back since leaving spontaneously in August.

The question that way heavy on their minds was what to do about Damon. They both knew David wouldn't approve of him being there at the celebration, nor would Jackie be welcomed. Their ex-daughter-in-law often invited herself to the family gatherings. She reasoned that they should welcome her, since her children were invited. To keep the children from being excluded, the family tolerated having her around. Yet, they knew David wouldn't want to see her.

A knock on the door surprised them, because they were not expecting anyone. Joseph stood up from his comfortable leather recliner to answer the door. Deloris wondered who could be knocking. Family members knew that they had an open-door policy, so it could be anyone. Most family members were always welcome. Consequently, the house was generally full of grandchildren, children, cousins, nieces, and nephews, who visit on the weekends.

Joseph walked back in the room with Damon following behind him. He had a grim look on his face. Their wayward son was the last person they expected to see.

Damon walked over to hug his mother, and then sat down on the couch opposite from them. As he sat down, a sigh escaped from his lips.

"Uh-oh," Deloris responded. "What's going on?" She knew he was up to something, and the sigh confirmed it.

Damon jumped straight to the subject. "I just found out that Dana is not my child," he replied, reaching over to hand the test results to his father.

Joseph and Deloris looked at each other knowingly. After Damon revealed his affair with Jackie and David had the children tested, the twins did not know that Deloris and Joseph didn't trust the DNA results.

Damon watched his parents' reaction; it wasn't what he had expected. Once the news was out that Jackie had a third man, he expected his parents to be livid, but they were calm.

His father spoke first. "Well, we could have told you that son," he said with a nonchalant tone. Joseph turned on the television to catch the rest of the NBA basketball game.

Damon's mouth dropped to the floor. "You knew, and you didn't tell me," he exclaimed, staring at his parents with disbelief. For the first time, he felt what betrayal feels like. He stood to leave. There was no explanation that could appease what they had done.

"Have a seat son," Joseph stood up to stop him from leaving. "Let us explain."

He wanted to object, but something kept him from moving. Reluctantly Damon sat back down.

"Your father and I didn't always know," Deloris interjected. "We kind of had an idea that the test results David received weren't accurate. But we can't tell you kids anything, so you wouldn't have believed us."

The couple had their doubts about Dana, but Ashley was definitely his because she and Tony look just alike. Both were born on the same day one year apart.

"Even if you can't trust science all the time son, you can trust God," Joseph said. "Science is human-run and humans make mistakes."

"That's right," Deloris put her hand up in affirmation. "Preach it, Joseph!"

Damon chuckled, understanding that his parents didn't think a third man was involved. Suddenly, he realized that Dana may be David's daughter after all. '*Oh, let it be,*' he said to himself silently, as Joseph continued preaching about trusting God.

"You know you children trust whatever the doctor tells you," Deloris said. "We know that you got to bow your head and call on the Almighty!"

"That's right, Deloris," Joseph agreed. "The *Lord* is the true doctor, the all-knowing."

Damon put his hand over his mouth to hide his grin. Every once in a while, his parents would have their own church service right in the living room. Once they got started, there was no stopping them.

"Hallelujah," Deloris proclaimed!

"Glory to God," Joseph shouted, lifting his hands into the air!

Damon decided to join in. "Thank you, Father," he said earnestly, as he thanked God that he came to speak with his parents first. Now, he could meet Jackie without accusing her. '*Who was he to condemn her anyway,*' Damon asked himself silently?

Still, he couldn't believe that his parents did not tell him that they didn't trust the initial test results. If they had spoken up, maybe David would have tested the children a second time. It certainly would have cut down on some of the drama. As he communicated his feelings to his parents, Deloris tried to explain.

"Sometimes, all you can do is pray for family," she said. "This situation was so hurtful to the entire family that we decided to just pray."

He sat and pondered what his mother said. It was true that there wasn't much anyone could say to make him deny a scientific test result in his hands. The past few months came to his mind, and Damon reflected on all that he'd put his family through. It helped him to grow, because he realized that actions have consequences.

Joseph's words broke Damon out of his reflection. "Now, it's time to try to heal these relationships," his father counseled him. He had taught his boys that forgiveness was the key to living a happier life. Damon nodded his head, as he listened to his father speak about the power of forgiveness.

Damon thought on his dad's words. His mind drifted back to when they were younger. Joseph's distant cousin had an unfaithful spouse. She came crying to his parents about her husband's betrayal. They advised her to stay married. Unfortunately, she couldn't get over it, because he slept with her best friend. He remembered it like it was yesterday. David and Damon were home when she walked into the living room crying. After she left, Joseph sat Chris, David, Damon and Derrick down to explain the importance of maintaining marital trust, difficulties arising from infidelity, and the power of forgiveness.

He looked up to find his parents staring at him, awaiting a response. Damon took a deep breath. "Thank you, Mom and Dad," he said. "I am going to go speak with Jackie."

"Alright son, we'll call and let David know that he needs to retake that test," Joseph said, standing up to hug his son. Deloris also walked with Damon to the doorway, hopeful for the first time in a long time that this miracle may help their family to heal.

Damon gave his parents another hug, and he left the house on the way to visit Jackie, Tony, Ashley and Dana.

Jackie had just received a text message from Damon that he was on the way to visit. She was busy tidying the house, and sent the children upstairs, who would pepper her with questions, if they knew Damon was coming to visit. She and Damon hadn't spoken since her blow up about Dominique. By now, she figured he had come to his senses and wanted to make amends. She'd been lonely, so she was happy that he was coming over. At the same time, his absence gave her time to reflect on what she needed in a relationship. She wished more than anything that she could turn back time and choose to work on her relationship with David, instead of seeking solace outside of her marriage.

After 15 years of marriage, David was still with her, even in his absence. She felt his gentle touch, and she could even smell his scent. Her memories were like visions, which came to her during the day and at night while she was dreaming. She had to forget the past, and move forward into a new and better future. She had to decide to live without regrets and focus on a new, better life. If only David would speak with her, perhaps she could help him understand. A smile crept across her face, as she dreamed of restarting a life with David again.

She heard a car door close in the distance, and the familiar beep from Damon turning on his car alarm. Jackie went to the door to greet him. From the look on Damon's face, he wasn't there to apologize. He was carrying something in his hands. It appeared to be a manila envelope. Jackie had no idea what that could mean. As Damon approached the door, she couldn't help but remember the look David had on his face, when he found out about her excessive spending. Even though they were fraternal twins, Damon reminded her of David in that moment.

When he reached the door, Jackie held out her arms to embrace him. He moved passed her with a quick hello. She stood looking at him, as he made his way to the couch. Damon plopped down. He was on the edge of his seat, his hands clasped together with a strange look on his face, and she was unable to decipher his emotions.

Reluctantly, Jackie walked away from the door to join Damon on the couch. As she sat beside him, he turned to hand her the papers that he was holding.

"What's this," she asked?

"Paternity results for Dana," he replied calmly.

"It seems that I am not her father," he said. "So, David may be the father, after all."

Jackie looked at the papers in her hands, and a feeling of hope welled up inside her. She gave Damon a half smile. Instinctively, they hugged one another. It wasn't the passionate hug of two lovers, but a comforting hug one friend gives to another, after overcoming a hard life challenge.

After about a minute, Damon chuckled. He looked down at the floor, and then raised his head to look at Jackie again all the while laughing. "This is actually a joyous occasion," he said.

Jackie tilted her head, then she cast her head down. Her eyes went up toward the ceiling and she started fidgeting. She shook her head as tears began to roll from her eyes. Damon hugged her again, and together they planned a way forward, hoping that David could forgive them both.

Inwardly, Damon was thrilled. They decided to wait to tell Dana, until David had a chance to retake the paternity test.

Sobs shook Jackie's body, and she held her hand to her mouth to muffle the noise. They had all been through so much. Finally, this good news could be just the catalyst the family needed to heal.

Tony came down the stairs. "Why are you crying, Mama," he asked?

He walked over to comfort his mother. Jackie started wiping her eyes. "Mommy is fine," she responded. Your father and I are having a conversation.

Tony turned to Damon. "What did you do to my mom," he asked? His fists were balled, and anger displayed across his face.

Jackie jumped up. "I'm fine, Tony," she said smiling. "These are tears of joy."

She smiled at her handsome, protective son, convincing him to go back upstairs.

Damon didn't say a word, until his son left the living room. "It's probably a good idea for us to keep our voices down," he said. "They don't need to know yet."

Jackie took a deep breath and sat back down on the couch. Tears started rolling down her face again. "So, what are we going to do?"

Damon explained that his parents were letting David know, and that he would probably take the test soon. He let her know that he would be there to co-parent Ashley and Tony and to help with Dana also when he could.

Somehow the two of them knew that Dana would have no problem accepting David as her father, after he retook the test.

"You are not alone," Damon told Jackie, taking her hand gently. "We are going to be here for you as a family. At the same time, I need you to understand that I am going to plan a future with Dominique's mother."

Jackie looked into Damon's eyes and noted his sincerity. They had both come to the same conclusion. The romantic relationship they shared, which started in a dark laundry room and under the cover of deception was over.

As Damon stood up to leave, he received a text message on his phone. He took a moment to read it, before walking upstairs to say goodbye to Tony, Ashley, and Dana. As he walked out of Jackie's home, Damon felt a gigantic weight lift from his body, and grinned from ear to ear. He sent a text back to Bridget to let her know he was on his way to see her.

David was working on his languages when he received a text message notification. He didn't usually receive messages from the family until later on in the day. Joseph had called to let him know that Damon wasn't Dana's father. So, he knew that he had to retake the paternity test.

His eyes diverted to the phone, and right away he knew who sent the message. Damon sent him a message to let him know that he'd broken things off with Jackie. Memories clouded his thoughts of the times spent with his brother. Like a movie playing in his mind, he saw the good times they shared with one another, including laughter, pranks, and conversations. As his mind continued down memory lane, another thought occurred to him. Why was he even thinking about his twin brother?

David scoffed. What did it matter to him? There was no way he was taking Jackie back after her betrayal. Even so, he looked at the message again. It gave him a sense of relief. He didn't read the rest of the message. His brother must have gotten a new number, because he'd blocked Damon's old number. *God you must be softening my heart,* he said to himself, because a few months ago, David certainly would have given Damon a piece of his mind.

Back in Michigan, Damon was grateful that his phone said that the message was sent to his brother was delivered. He wasn't sure if David would read it or not. He purchased another phone, just so that he could send the message. He wanted David to be the first to know that he and Jackie were no longer together.

After he left Jackie, Damon felt a lightness in his body and mind. In the comfort of Bridget's home, he had time to think to himself. Things were starting to come together. For the first time in nearly a year, he felt like he was making the right decisions. He no longer felt like a user or a cheat. If he'd known the stress that he felt all those years would leave so quickly, he may have left Jackie sooner.

Bridget and Dominique rode with Damon on the way to his parents' house, so he could let them know what he and Jackie had decided. They would co-parent Tony and Ashley and remain friends. His heart ached for his brother David; he didn't deserve all the pain Damon had put him through. What could he do to heal the relationship? How could he fix things? He talked to Bridget about it, as they rode in the car. She opened the glove compartment, taking out the pocket Bible, which she had given him. Turning to the book of Philippians, she read quietly as he drove. "Do not be anxious about anything," Bridget began. "…by prayer and petition, with thanksgiving, present your requests to God."

Chapter 18

In the present...

Georgia

David spent most of the day talking to his family back home. They filled him in on what has been happening with everyone including Jackie, Damon, and the children. He wasn't too concerned about his brother or ex-wife but interested in what the children were doing. All of the sports and activities were on pause, because there wasn't anyone around to take them back and forth with both parents working so many hours.

He learned that Dana busied herself by trying to earn money by selling items online. She had apologized to her parents for her behavior, but still kept Damon at a distance. Tony and Ashley argued most of the time, especially when they played video games together

David and the twins miss the family back in Michigan. He made plans to visit his family this summer as soon as school let out. The twins would still have plenty of time with the family, because David was leaving them there for the entire summer break.

While they're away, he could spend more time with April. It was so easy being with her. He didn't have to fight with her or second guess himself about how to make her happy. She was easy to please, and he couldn't believe how simple it was to satisfy her. April was on her way over. David didn't want her to drive, so he ordered her an Uber ride to bring her to his house. Meanwhile, he fried fish and prepared the house for her arrival.

David was hosting a bid whist party with fish, fries, pizza, non-alcoholic beverages, cake, and pie. Junior and Nakita were allowed to invite friends over for a spades card party. The festivities were starting around seven o'clock. Some of the twins' friends arrived early, but David didn't mind. He decided to save the food, until most of the people had arrived. He also made it very clear that gambling was not allowed. The twins already knew, but David would make it known to their friends. If they couldn't abide by the rules, then they would have to leave and will not be welcomed back.

As the musical notes from the front doorbell rang, Nakita yelled that she would answer the door. David hoped it was April, because she should be here right about now. David could hear voices at the door, but couldn't make out who it was. He focused back on the fish. Before he knew it, someone had covered his eyes with their hands. He smiled for he knew exactly who it was. David grabbed the hands on his eyes and turned around to see April was standing there with a big grin. She looked beautiful as ever and her fragrant, rose-scented perfume smelled good.

"Muffin, you made it," David winked at her.

"Muffin," she repeated, thinking about the name he'd given her. "I like it," she smiled.

"Yes, I am here, and thank you for the ride although I really could have driven myself."

David turned away from the stove to wrap April in his arms. "Hey you," he said softly. She smiled in response and just as they were about to kiss, Nakita came into the kitchen with a friend.

"Now children you mustn't do things like that," Nakita and her friend giggled.

Both David and April chuckled as well.

"Who do we have here," David asked?

"Dad I would like for you to meet my best friend, Laila."

"Hello Laila," David said, stretching out his arm to shake her hand.

"Hi Mr. Campbell, thanks for letting us come over."

"You're welcome."

"And this is my dad's girlfriend April," Nakita introduced April.

After exchanging pleasantries, more guests began to arrive and the house was filling up fast with people ready to play games and eat. April helped David get the food ready, as the twins took the guests jackets to hang up. David looked forward to an evening full of fun and laughter, because his family needed it.

In the present...

Michigan

Jackie grabbed the test results, hopped in her car, and drove to her mother's place. Tears were steadily streaming down her face, making visibility difficult especially since it was nighttime. She had to speak to her mother face to face. Leaving Dana in charge probably was a mistake, but she couldn't help herself.

She and Damon finally resolved the relationship. In the past, he told her that he loved her and hated that she was with David, his brother. Now the opportunity finally arrived for them to be together, and they both decided to end the relationship. It was the right thing to do, but the decision still left Jackie with feelings of uncertainty about her future.

Finally, the senior towers were in view. Jackie whipped her car into an empty space and hurriedly walked to her mother's apartment. The front desk clerk noticed her and opened the door. Jackie walked straight through to the elevator, saying a barely audible thank you as she passed.

When she reached Bernice's door, she pounded louder than she expected, as she tried to get her emotions under control. She had a key, but in her distress, she didn't think to use it.

Bernice opened the door with a look of terror on her face. Her eyes lit up when she realized it was Jackie and her eyes became saddened when she saw the tears rolling down her daughter's face. "Jackie," Bernice said with a concerned look on her face.

"Mama," Jackie responded, quickly embracing her mother. Bernice wrapped her arms around her daughter. Together, they walked to the couch. The sobs were harder and louder now that she was in her mother's arms.

Bernice desperately wanted to know what happened to make her daughter cry so hard. She waited patiently until Jackie gained her composure. The suspense was killing her. The longer they sat quiet, the more Jackie cried. Finally, Bernice decided to question Jackie to find out what was troubling her.

"What happened," Bernice asked? "Did David say something foul to you? Did he compare you to that thing he's trying to be with? I'll kill him if he thinks he's going to hurt my baby verbally. No good dirty bastard."

Jackie pulled away from her to try to answer, but all she could do was shake her head no. The tears and sobs hadn't stopped either. She just wanted to let it all out. Jackie leaned back into her mother's arms and the weeping started again.

Bernice sighed. She continued to rub and pat Jackie's back as her daughter let it all out. *'I don't know who hurt my daughter, but I swear I'm going to make sure he wishes he was never born,'* Bernice was in her own little world mumbling to herself, until Jackie called out to her.

"Mama," Jackie exclaimed! "You're supposed to be consoling me." Jackie exclaimed, looking up at her mother! "What are you mumbling about?"

Bernice scoffed. "I'm not ignoring what you're going through, I'm angry that you've been hurt," she replied.

Jackie thought about that for a minute. She stopped sobbing, and she explained to her mother what happened. Her hope was that David would come to his senses, and they could repair their 15-year marriage. She felt a sense of failure, because she'd ruined her marriage for a relationship that did not work out.

Bernice was glad her daughter stopped balling, so she could finally get some answers. "Now, what's in the envelope?"

Jackie had forgotten the envelope, which she grasped tightly in her hands.

"It's the test results," Jackie explained. "Damon is not Dana's father and the Campbell's believe the lab made an error with the first DNA test."

"What are you talking about," Bernice gawked?

Jackie stood up and started pacing. She gave her mother the rundown of what took place when Damon brought over the test results. After she explained everything, she sat back down. The two of them looked at the manila test results together.

"Have you looked at it?" Bernice asked.

Jackie nodded her head. "He said Dana wasn't his," Jackie responded.

"I guess the better question is, is it true," she queried? "And what about Ashley?" Bernice thought about her last question. Ashley and Tony both looked like Damon. When they were born no one thought anything about it, because David and Damon are twins.

Jackie didn't answer right away. "I've only been with David and Damon, and Ashley is definitely Damon's daughter" she confirmed.

Her mother's expression let her know that she couldn't hide the truth. "Oh Jackie, this is good news," her mother exclaimed, excited that the plan she started months ago to bring Jackie and David back together was working like a charm. She was getting help from on High, because not even Bernice could have thought of Dana being David's child, after all.

Bernice smiled and hugged Jackie closely. She explained to Jackie that now was the time for her to begin preparing herself and the children to see David. Surely, he'd have to come visit soon. When he came, they must be ready to see him. She looked at her daughters disheveled hairdo and the few pounds she'd packed on in the last year.

"Girl, you've got to get it together," Bernice said. "When David arrives, you've got to look the best he's ever seen you."

Bernice stood up and grabbed both of Jackie's arms. "Stop all this crying," she counseled her daughter. "This is good news."

Jackie slowly moved out of Bernice's grasp. "Well, thank you for supporting me," Jackie replied while reflecting on her mother's words

Bernice continued to advise her daughter. One thing Bernice knew about was how to get a man. She embraced her daughter to let her know that she was going to help her get David back. Jackie looked at the determined look in Bernice's eyes and believed her.

David's personal cell phone rang. The ringtone was the general tone, so it wasn't April or his parents. He was still busy studying, and the interruption annoyed him slightly. *Who could this be?* He walked over to pick up the phone. It was Micki calling, which was unusual considering it was still during working hours. So, he decided to answer and put it on speaker. "Hey Micki, what's going on," he asked.

"Hey, have you heard from Damon," Micki replied in a joyful tone.

David shook his head; she was calling to gossip or gloat. "Yeah, I did," David said.

"So, you heard the news about him and Jackie," Micki asked?

He rolled his eyes. "I know you're happy, and you couldn't stand the two of them together," David replied. Micki didn't have anything important to share, and he was ready to end the call when she spoke again.

"Is that all he told you," she asked again? She figured David hadn't the foggiest idea of what Damon revealed to the family. Micki wanted to hear his reaction to the fact that Dana was not Damon's daughter.

"He sent another text, but I didn't care to read it," David replied.

"Well, here's the clincher," Micki offered. "Damon has a baby with another woman named Bridget."

David stopped in his tracks. "What are you talking about," David exclaimed?

"Well, dear brother," Micki explained. "It seems that Damon has fallen in love with someone named Bridget, and the two of them are getting married."

He couldn't tell if his sister was for real or playing with him. "Seriously," David responded? It was hard for David to envision Damon married. He heard from his parents that his brother had started selling dinners that he cooked on the weekends, worked in the factory during the day, and helped to take care of the children.

"I mean just what I said," Micki continued. "Jackie and Damon are done for good."

"Gratitude swelled up within him," as he fell to his knees and started weeping, thanking, and praising God. He wasn't sure that he believed that Damon and Jackie were done when his brother texted him. David was surprised at how much the news that his brother was getting married gave him joy.

Micki was floored at David's jubilant reaction. She wanted to get David riled, so they could trash Jackie together and run her name in the ground. She just wanted to gossip about her, but hearing her brother praising God threw her for a loop. '*I can't believe him; ain't that about nothing,*' she thought.

David could hear Micki continuing to gossip through the phone. He didn't care about what she was saying and said goodbye, disconnecting the call, as he continued to give thanks.

Chapter 19

Jackie could hardly contain her excitement. She was overjoyed to learn that David and the twins were coming back home for the summer. All of her plans backfired on her. Nothing that she and Damon talked about came to pass. She needed an outlet. After all she's been through, her love for David started to grow. The more she pondered on the life she once had, the more Jackie knew that her relationship with David had to be fixed. It was decided, David had to be hers again. The reality dawned on her that she really felt deep affection for him. Why else would she not want him to know about Damon? Her infidelity wasn't because she hated him. Jackie hoped that they could learn to communicate better, so that she could express when his actions made her angry or frustrated her, and they could work through it together.

Suddenly, her mind shifted to April. Micki told Jackie's sister, Jada that David is bringing April with him. The thought of meeting David's new romantic interest, sent Jackie into a fit of jealousy. *I'm going to get my man back, if it's the last thing I do.* A determined look crept across her face. She knew exactly what needed to be done, time alone with David to talk. As her thoughts turned to the twins, Jackie called Junior on his cell phone to check on him and Nakita.

In the back of the SUV, David heard Junior's cell phone ring. "Hi Mom," Junior said. "We're on the way." As they spoke, David navigated the vehicle onto the expressway for the long drive north to his home state. He, April, Aunt Gladys and the twins fit comfortably in the expansive seating room of his vehicle. His aunt let it be known from the get-go that she was not driving, but April volunteered to help.

In the past, when a trip was taken that required driving instead of flying, he was the only driver. His ex-wife only drove locally, and she wasn't comfortable driving on the highway for a long period or in unfamiliar territory. He would drive for as long as he could, and then they would find a hotel for the night. David believed that she just didn't want to drive, so he appeased her.

They started the drive at midnight. If everything went as planned, they would arrive in Pontiac, Michigan by 3 p.m. Aunt Gladys made chicken salad sandwiches, so there wasn't a need to stop for food. They'd only planned to stop for gas, restroom breaks and to switch drivers.

The twins were excited to go home to see their mother and siblings. The family was in Atlanta for Christmas, but Jackie and the kids didn't come.

As they hit the road, the group experienced smooth sailing when they pulled away from David's home in Lilburn. Aunt Gladys had her son bring her up right after the morning rush. She was so excited to travel that she arrived very early. Her family experienced the restlessness, so they figured if Gladys was with the people with whom she was traveling, it would calm her down a bit. That didn't bother David, because he loved having his aunt around.

David took the first leg. He hopped on I-85 southward to I-285 west, then they would merge onto I-75 north, which will take them all the way to Pontiac. The drive will take through Tennessee, Kentucky, and Ohio.

The family started out talking and laughing, until Aunt Gladys fell asleep. Everyone else followed suit. He was especially happy when April dozed off, so she wouldn't be tired when it was time for her to take the wheel. In the rear, Nakita finished speaking with her mother and hung up the phone.

Jackie was so ecstatic that David was bringing them. It was Friday before Memorial Day, and her twins were coming home for the summer. They would leave to go back the first of August, because schools started earlier in Georgia. She wanted to see them all. It didn't matter that he was accompanied by April. Once he saw how delighted she was to see him, Jackie hoped that his focus would be on her, not April.

Her attempts to speak with David on the phone, after the breakup with Damon were unwelcome. He rebuffed all of her advances. She hated to see the children's lives turned upside down. Fortunately, she was able to find a good job and could now afford to take care of them in the way they had become accustomed.

David may even be surprised by her enthusiasm toward him. Treating him kindly had always gained his attention in the past. Following her mother's advice, Jackie worked out daily to get her body back in shape. She wore the red summer dress that David bought her in New York. The weather was still a bit chilly in Michigan at night, but they would be indoors. Her mother gave her a beautiful shawl to wrap around her shoulders.

Jackie kept checking her phone. Nakita agreed to text her mother along the route from Georgia to Michigan and let her know once they arrived. Jackie sent Deloris a text, letting her know that she would be on her way as soon as Nakita confirmed that they had arrived at David's parents' home. David still didn't want to see his brother, and only time will tell how long it will take them to heal the discord between them.

At the Campbell's home, Deloris was busy in the kitchen preparing the side dishes for the family when Jackie's text caused her cell phone to buzz. Her son was driving home with her twin grandchildren. She would do anything to see them more often. As her children grew up, her biggest concern was that they would want to leave the state. David was the first to leave, his departure saddened both she and Joseph.

She knew Damon would surely grace the family with his presence, even if David didn't want him to come over. She heard the patio door open. Joseph carried another batch of meat in from the grill. He smiled at her when their eyes met. She returned the smile. They both knew what each other was thinking. The light was beaming in both of their eyes. This was a glorious day for Deloris and her husband.

They prayed that everyone remained respectful, so they could get through the day without any drama.

When they heard a car door slam outside the house, she and Joseph looked at each other in excitement. Before they could move an inch, the doorbell rang. Deloris shouted in praise and thanksgiving, running to the door. She flung it opened and was greeted by five beaming faces.

Nakita and Junior were the first to walk in and hug their granny. Then, they both ran to papa. Gladys and Deloris rocked side to side, as they embraced. Joseph hugged April, as David wrapped his mother in the tightest embrace. In that moment, he realized how much he missed being close to his family.

After the greetings, the men went outside to grill the rest of the meat. In the kitchen, the ladies joked and laughed while helping Deloris with the rest of the food. A few hours later, the family started arriving. The twins were happy to see everyone, but their mother and siblings hadn't arrived yet. Nakita sent a text to her mother to see what was keeping them.

Everyone heard Dana, Ashley, and Tony in the driveway, as they hopped out of their mother's car. Nakita and Junior ran out the house to greet them.

Deloris stepped to David, "I could send her away if you want," she offered. She really didn't want to disappoint the twins, but she didn't want David or April to be uncomfortable either.

"No Mama, it's okay," David responded, grabbing April's hand. "April and I have already discussed Jackie." He looked at April and winked at her. Together, they walked outside to meet David's ex-wife.

Jackie became excited, when she saw David walking toward them. He and April were holding hands, but that wasn't going to stop her from going after what she wanted. The twins ran to hug their mother, before focusing their attention on Ashley, Tony and Dana. After the focus was completely off of her, she made her move.

She walked over to David to give him a hug, but he held up his left hand to stop her. April's hand was still in his right hand. Jackie moved forward to wrap her arms around him anyway, but this time he stepped back and pulled his girlfriend in front of him. "Jackie, I'd like for you to meet April," he said politely. "April, this is the twins' mother, Jackie."

April reached out her hand to shake Jackie's hand. "Hi Jackie, how are you," April asked, giving Jackie a genuine smile? She'd heard so much about her, and April felt she knew her just a little bit.

Jackie reluctantly stuck out her hand. She barely grasped April's hand and quickly released it.

"Daddy, I missed you." Dana grabbed him around his waist, as she's always done. That was the break Jackie needed. He and April's hands came apart. Even though, the children were around them, Jackie hopped between David and April. 'I've missed you too, my big teddy bear." That was the nickname she had for him.

David was immediately offended, as his main concern was April. He gave her a displeased look. April came up behind him, and David swiftly moved away from his ex-wife and joined hands with April. "What are you doing Jackie," he asked?

She scoffed. "I'm just trying to tell you how much I've missed you," Jackie explained, ignoring the fact that he held tightly to April's hand.

He interrupted her before she finished speaking. "I am going to ask you once to respect my Muffin for the remainder of your time at my parents' home," he said sternly.

Deloris motioned for the children to go in the house. She could see an argument brewing. This was exactly why she didn't want Jackie around. Any fool could see that she'd finally realized what they'd all told her from the beginning. She was crazy to let David go.

Jackie was shocked, and her hands went to her chest. "Did you just say Muffin," she asked, referring to the nickname that he gave

April? All those years together, he never gave her a nickname. Sometimes he would say Jack just to shorten her name even more, but that was it.

"I didn't mumble, you heard me correctly," he said.

Jackie turned away from the couple. He was more into April, than she'd anticipated. It was going to be a challenge to win his heart again. She loved a good challenge.

The two walked back into the house. She allowed them to walk away without a comeback. This was a game changer, not for her to give up but to intensify her pursuit. April may have won him now, but Jackie was sure she'd be the victor in the end.

After the ordeal with Jackie was over, the family resumed their fellowship together. Although no one wanted Jackie around, it was too painful to send her away because of the children. If she left, then she'd take her children home as well. No one wanted to exclude them, so the Campbells tolerated her presence. To everyone's surprise, she remained quiet the entire time.

April kept close watch on Jackie. David focused all his attention on Muffin, because he didn't expect Jackie to come on to him the way that she did. He asked April several times, if she was ok. She had to reassure him that she was fine.

She thought about Leslie who is currently dating her ex-husband. Even after she'd won his affection, she would do subtle things to brag. They would consequently meet in the hallway at work; Leslie would either reach for Robbie's hand, or if they were seated in proximity, Leslie would run her hand somewhere on Robbie, as long as it was visible to her. At first, it bothered her, but she didn't let on that it was hurtful. This was a walk in the park compared to her own drama with her ex-husband. Even so, David clung to her hand.

They were seated around the house, eating the delicious food Deloris and Joseph prepared. April, Aunt Gladys, and Nakita helped, but Deloris did most of the work. Joseph cooked all the meat on the grill, including ribs, chicken, hamburger patties, and hot dogs. There was an abundance of food left when everyone finished eating, enough for leftovers for almost everyone.

Before the family ate, Joseph led the family in prayer. The cliché is a family that prays together stays together. The Campbells were definitely together. April enjoyed being in their company. Everyone got along well, just like her family.

After the food was eaten and the kitchen cleaned. Everyone migrated to the living room. The children were upstairs, as usual. April sat next to David on the couch. He began to rub the back of her neck while continuously apologizing for Jackie's actions.

"It's ok, you were with me the whole time," she responded to him, enjoying the neck rub. That statement seemed to satisfy him, and a smile as broad as the ocean came upon his face.

After an exciting game of Scattegories, everyone decided to leave for the evening. Jackie asked David to drive the twins home while she toted the other three. Joseph offered to help, but David agreed to drive. This was a chance for David to clear the air.

April didn't know what Jackie's love life was like. David never offered any information and she never questioned him about her.

"Oh girl, I know my brother, and when he's through with something or someone, he's done," Micki said, giving April a reassuring smile, as David followed Jackie and the children out the door.

Walking outside into the warm evening air, David felt comfortable with the familiarity of leaving his parents' house with Jackie and the children. He stopped in his tracks at the sight of his brother Damon, standing next to his car with a young lady and a baby. Damon stepped forward and introduced Bridget to David.

"Bridget, this is my brother, David and his...um...this is Jackie," Damon said nervously, gesturing toward his brother and Jackie. David stuck out his hand, but Bridget leaned forward to give him a hug.

"Dave, man I also wanted you to meet my son Dominique. He was both nervous and embarrassed. At that moment, Micki, her husband, Chris and his family came out of the house, curiously surveying the unfolding drama in front of them.

David looked at Damon's son and then at Bridget. He stepped forward to take Dominique in his arms.

"So, this is the nephew I've heard so much about," he said, as Dominique giggled. "Congratulations to both of you."

Everyone was waiting for an eruption that never happened. Micki had returned to the house to get Deloris and Joseph. Their parents came to the front door, ready to break up the fight, if it occurred.

"It's late, you stayed out here all this time," David said.

Damon shrugged his shoulders. "Yeah, pretty much."

"Son why did you subject them to that," Deloris couldn't believe he'd have them sit in a car for hours waiting. "You could have at least sent Bridget and Dominique in, if you wanted something to eat. There's plenty of food, if you're hungry."

"No, we didn't come to eat," Damon explained. "We drove around the neighborhood, while we waited." A nervous laugh came roaring from his mouth.

"Well, you've seen everybody," David interjected. As he turned toward the house, he saw April standing at the door with Aunt Gladys. She was a ray of sunshine. Memories of the betrayal came rushing back to him. He couldn't leave April by herself. "Muffin," he called out to her. "Let's roll." David and April got into his SUV to drive to the hotel. Deloris ushered the children back in the house. Jackie stood at the edge of the driveway alone, as a single tear flowed down the side of her face.

Jackie was mortified that Damon showed up and with that baby. Her plans didn't go well. The thought that David had given April a cutesy nickname was bothersome. Why didn't he give her one? He was so much in love with her, but he didn't do that for her. It suddenly hit her that she probably wouldn't have liked a nickname She simply did not appreciate all that he did for her, until she didn't have it. "David, I'm sorry," Jackie cried out into the darkness, her voice echoing over the trees.

Family members were preparing to leave, when they heard Jackie's high-pitched scream. The noise stopped them in their tracks. Tears started rolling down Jackie's face. She stood alone crying.

"Here we go," Chris spoke sarcastically. No one wanted to deal with Jackie's outburst, especially at this hour. It was well after midnight. The neighborhood was quiet, and there was barely any noise from the neighbors.

Damon and Micki both left with their families. Joseph invited Jackie in the house to compose herself, before she drove home. Dana, Ashley, and Tony protested, because they wanted to spend the night. The girls ended up sleeping upstairs. Junior and Tony went to the basement to give their aunt the room they usually occupy. Deloris prepared the other guest room for Jackie.

Deloris could hear Jackie crying during the night. For the first time, she realized how difficult the entire situation was on Jackie and felt sympathy for her.

Reality set in, and Jackie realized she was alone. Tears streamed down her face, wetting the pillows beneath her. Everybody in her world had a significant other in their life, except her. She'd given up her family and had nothing to show for it. Both of her brothers were dating now, and even defiant Jada had found someone. Damon and David both moved on. She detested the thought of ending up living alone like her mother.

Jackie heard a noise at the door and turned her head just in time to see Aunt Gladys come into the room. She sat on the white, wooden rocking chair across from Jackie's bed, as she turned on the night light. Even though Jackie had caused her nephew pain, the lady clearly needed help. Gladys was in God's blessing business. No matter what happened, God wasn't going out of business. A soft, gospel melody moved through the room, as Gladys parted her lips to sing, "Angels watching over me," she crooned quietly. Instantly, Jackie felt better, closing her eyes as Gladys' soulful, soprano voice floated through the air. Gladys returned to her room, as Jackie floated off to sleep.

Chapter 20

Since this was April's first time in Michigan, David wanted to show her as many of the popular places as possible. The plan was for it to be just the two of them, but the five children begged him to take them along. As he thought about it, they really hadn't planned much for them. David didn't mind, as long as April was good with the idea. April was fine with it, and Jackie agreed to let the children go.

He started the tour in Oakland County. The first spot was the Palace, then they visited the mall. He wanted to get out and walk so April could see all the stores. David had to instruct everyone that this was only a window-shopping trip. If April wanted something, he would get it for her but after the children weren't around.

After the mall, they toured Eastern Michigan University in Ypsilanti and visited the University of Michigan in Ann Arbor. David took her to see Michigan Stadium, nicknamed the Big House, where the U of M football team plays. The stadium seats over 100,000 people and is the largest in the U.S., third largest in the world.

As long as he'd lived in Michigan, they'd never attended a game in person. The family were all Wolverines fans, but they preferred to watch the games on television. David turned his head toward April to gauge her expression. She appeared to be enjoying herself with the five children included. Each spoke to April respectfully and engaged her in their conversations. Even though they didn't expect all the children to come, the day was going great.

The family stopped at a local sub shop for April to try its unique, delicious submarine sandwiches. This sub restaurant was only in the state of Michigan. David and the twins missed the food very much. April ordered the same submarine sandwich that David wanted, a six-inch pizza burger sub. Everyone had a combo meal with fries and a drink.

After lunch, they headed to downtown Detroit, passing the Detroit Metro Airport on the way. He gave her the history of the changes to the airport and pointed out the exit where a plane crashed back in 1987. As David continued April's tour, the children fell asleep, so he kept the history and past news events going.

A giant Uniroyal tire came into view on the east side of the freeway. It stands 80 feet tall and was once a Ferris wheel at the New York World's Fair. April was amazed at the attraction, because she had never seen a tire so large. It loomed over the interstate highway in Allen Park, Michigan.

As they made their way to the Lodge Freeway heading south. David continued to give her the history of the region. As they drove through a tunnel, he explained to her that they were driving under what was known as Cobo Hall a convention center in the city. It had been renamed as TCF Center.

After they emerged from the tunnel, Hart Plaza was on their right. The Detroit River was in view as well as Ontario, Canada across the water. Hart Plaza is a destination and venue for festivals, special events, and concerts along the riverfront. When he was younger, David's parents would pack all five of them in the station wagon with drinks, chips and sandwiches to watch the fireworks at night at Hart Plaza. It was an all-day event. People from all over the metro area would come downtown on the last Wednesday in June. The Detroit fireworks were a spectacular show.

After leaving the tunnel, David navigated the vehicle on Lodge freeway, which turned into Jefferson Avenue. He showed the family Joe Louis' fist and the Spirit of Detroit statue. As time slipped away, David realized that they needed to return home, because he had something special planned for April.

When they arrived, Jackie was still at the Campbell's residence. Deloris tried to get her to go home, but she wouldn't leave. Why would she leave, when David had all the children with him? They were bound to come back any minute. As long as he was back in town, Jackie clearly planned on hanging around.

Bernice and Deloris were in the kitchen. David had something special going on so she and Bernice wanted to know what it was. Jackie sat with Aunt Gladys in the living room on the couch. "Do you know what David is planning," she inquired innocently? She knew Aunt Gladys probably wouldn't disclose any information, but it was worth a shot.

Aunt Gladys looked up from her crossword puzzle she was working on and peered at Jackie from the top of her glasses. "Now what makes you think he has something special going on?"

"I overheard Deloris talking to someone," Jackie replied.

"Well, if that's the case, I'm sure it doesn't involve you," Gladys said gently. The Campbell family didn't beat around the bush, and someone had to let her know she shouldn't pry into David's affairs.

The truth hurt, and those words cut deep. However, Jackie wasn't willing to give up just yet. "Do you think I have a chance with him again," Jackie inquired, her eyes imploring Aunt Gladys to answer positively? She wanted to ask David, but needed someone who wasn't afraid to tell her the truth.

Aunt Gladys put down her puzzle, grabbed Jackie by her hands, and looked intently in her eyes. "Jackie, you...," she began and stopped herself. Gladys started again, "we are in control of our own destiny honey, but the other person has to be in agreement when relationships are involved."

Gladys spoke with Jackie about how to pray for forgiveness. "Self-condemnation is one of the most powerful ways to destroy a life," she explained to Jackie. "David won't be able to forgive you, until you forgive yourself. David can't love you again, until you learn to love yourself, as God loves you."

"Stop asking people what to do, Jackie" Gladys said. "The good book says, come to me all who are weary and burdened." Jackie listened intently, as Gladys spoke to her about getting up early in the morning for worship and seeing her family whole again. Prayer was the only advice she could give, Jackie. All kinds of conflicting thoughts were in Gladys' spirit, but her relationship with Christ prevented her from allowing those words to come out.

Jackie pondered Gladys' advice for a minute, before hearing David's voice in the kitchen. "Well, he's back now," Gladys said.

"You know my stomach isn't feeling too good," Jackie said. "I think I'll go upstairs and lie down." She grabbed her stomach, as she slowly walked up the stairs.

David made it back to his parents' house around 4 p.m. to drop off the children. He and April went back to the hotel to relax, before meeting up with the family again that evening. David planned a big surprise for April.

However, what he didn't expect was Jackie and Bernice to be present. He told Aunt Gladys to leave them be. If they wanted to attend, it was okay. They were in for a rude awakening. He laughed to himself. Since the two of them wanted to play games, then he would go toe to toe with them. Tonight, was going to be an awesome event.

He advised April to get some rest, and then freshen up for dinner later. She slept in the van on their way back to Pontiac. The children had awakened, so they'd kept David company as he drove them back to his parents' home.

After resting for a bit, April and David prepared for the evening. David was hopeful that everything was going to work out well. They headed back to his parents' house in the evening. As he sat in the living room, a text message came through to let him know that the guests were very close to his parents' house.

"Who's that," April asked, teasingly? She usually didn't care who he was texting, because he always disclosed that information on his own.

The question startled him. He thought she was in the kitchen with his mother and aunt. "Oh, just some people we know," David replied. It wasn't a lie; he just didn't tell her exactly who it was.

The doorbell rang, and David rushed to open the door. His special guests had arrived on time. He welcomed them into his parents' home.

April couldn't believe her eyes, as she watched her family members, including both parents walk into the house. She was totally unaware they were coming to Michigan. She ran to them, "hey what are you all doing here?" She smiled happily; it was a pleasant surprise to see them.

"We were invited, sweetie," her mother Angela replied.

"Invited," April asked curiously. "By whom?"

"By David silly, who else could it be," her mother was all smiles as she spoke?

She turned to David curiously. "You didn't tell me you were bringing my family to town."

"Well, you know me; I like surprises," he replied, smiling and raising his eyebrows twice in a playful manner.

The rest of the clan made their way into the house. April gleefully introduced her family to everyone. Her tone changed just a little when she got to Jackie and Bernice, but she was still ecstatic to have her folks.

David was joyful to see April excited. The catering company arrived with the food. He deliberately ordered a smaller amount of prime rib, macaroni and cheese, yams, green beans, potatoes, rolls and apple pie for dessert all of which is April's favorite. He did that just in case Bernice and Jackie tried to force their way in. He was determined to not have them partake in the meal, but they were more than welcome to stay and mingle. It wasn't the Christian thing to do, but he wasn't playing games. Tonight, was a serious night, and they had no business getting involved. The catering was for the adults only, and they ordered pizza for the children. If they were hungry, they could eat what the children ate.

April stood next to David. "What is this that you've done," she asked him?

"Oh, I just wanted you to have a nice time, and spoil you with your favorite food." He gently grabbed her hand. "I know it hasn't been that long since we've ate, that's why I suggested you not eat all of your lunch."

"I see, it's a good thing I listened." She sweetly gazed in his eyes. "Thank you for this. It's been a long while since I've vacationed with all of my family."

They tenderly embraced.

Micki spoke out, "David, I haven't seen you this happy in a very long time." She was throwing shade to Jackie and Bernice.

The family nodded in agreement. All the family was in awe of what David had planned. He always went above and beyond to please his lady. April and her parents appreciated the things David has done and continually do for her.

The pizza arrived shortly after the adult's meal. David explained to Jackie and Bernice that he didn't include them in the adult meal. He offered them the pizza, which they both reluctantly accepted. Everyone was on the ground level eating and talking just as last night.

David, April, and both sets of parents sat at the dining room table. The younger children were at the kitchen table, as usual. The teenagers and preteens were scattered around the house like everyone else. April's sisters and brothers-in-laws interacted with Micki and Chris'.

Before everyone was finished eating, David stood up and called for everyone to the dining room, kids and all. He gently motioned for April to stand up, and she agreed without hesitation.

When everyone was in the dining area or as close to it as they could, he started speaking. "I just want to thank everyone for coming and meeting with April and I. I've truly missed all of you. This is an amazing family and what would make it even more amazing is this beautiful lady standing next to me."

April gasped in surprise. He was thanking her for being in his life and making it known to his family.

"April Denice White Lockhart, my Muffin, I love you very, very much. Nothing would make me happier than you doing me the honor of walking beside me forever," David gushed, dropping down to one knee. He pulled a box from his pants pocket and opened it up. "Will you marry me?"

Tears sprang in her eyes. How could this be? He never let on that he was thinking about getting married. David was full of surprises. She couldn't speak, the word yes was in her mind, but she couldn't get it out.

Chris interrupted the momentum. "She's speechless," he said.

The family laughed but waited with anticipation.

April laughed nervously, noticing Jackie frowning out of the corner of her eye and Dana looking down at the carpet.

"Say yes honey." Her father spoke out. They adored David and was grateful for him bringing happiness in her life.

April looked David in his eyes, before dropping down on her knees to speak with him. "It has been about a year since you left Michigan," she said. "Are you sure you're ready?" David nodded his head. "Yes," April conceded, hugging him tightly.

David jumped to his feet and lifted April in the air. A round of applause and whistling was going on. The twins were the first to congratulate David and April. The four of them shared a group hug, as the rest of the family continued to roar their approval and excitement.

Not everyone was happy about the engagement. Jackie and Bernice were blindsided. He proposed to April right in front of their faces.

When David dropped to his knee, they knew what was coming. Jackie wanted to interrupt, but Micki sealed her mouth with her hand. Her other hand was on the back of her neck. She started to bite her, but Micki's hand became tighter around her neck. There was nothing she could do but cry.

After the family quieted down, Micki spoke to the unwanted guests. "See what happens when you invite yourself. You get your hand handed to you on a platter." She laughed, as she walked away.

Bernice caught David by himself. "David are you sure this is…"

"This doesn't concern you, Bernice. And we've already had this discussion in Atlanta. I don't care what you and Jackie want. This is my life, and I don't have to answer to either of you." He walked away before she could get another word in.

Deloris walked to both of them and escorted them out of her house. Jackie took her children with her, but Junior and Nakita stayed with their dad.

Damon made his way inside, as Jackie, Bernice, and the children were coming out. He could tell that the two women were upset. His mother probably dismissed them from her home. He hoped he didn't get the same treatment.

"You manage to arrive way after the surprise event." Jackie was attacking him with her words.

"I'll keep the children, if you want," he replied, not wanting to argue.

"Fine by me," Jackie agreed, as she walked to the car.

"Dana, Ashley, Tony, you can stay with me," Damon offered, watching his children and Dana return to the front door.

Jackie stared in the direction of the front door. A portion of her wanted to curse Damon out for his role in breaking up her marriage. She thought better of it, because Deloris, Aunt Gladys and Joseph would eat her alive if she went back in the house. "Get in the car," Jackie said to her mother, as she slammed the car door.

"What's he doing here," David asked his mother, as Damon walked in with Bridget and Dominique?

"I called him," she explained.

David took a step back to look at his mother.

She shrugged her shoulders. "You two need to talk. I had no idea you were going to propose to April tonight, because you told me you were going to do it when you got back to Atlanta."

"I wanted everyone to be surprised," he sighed. "That's why her family is here." It was a long time coming. The Lord had been pressing on his heart to make amends with his brother. He had every intention of doing just that but not tonight.

He thought about a sermon that he heard from a couple of months ago. The pastor preached on forgiveness. He informed the congregation that harboring ill feelings were not only sinful but harmful to the body. Moreover, forgiveness was for the individual, not the person forgiven. Lastly, if you couldn't forgive others, then God wouldn't forgive you. He wrestled with that word for weeks. How can he forgive his brother, when he did the unthinkable?

David wanted to grow higher in his relationship with God. When the pastor and First Lady shifted, the congregation should shift as well. When it's time for elevation, he wanted to be in position to be blessed and be a blessing. David watched his brother, as he made his way through the family. He didn't put forth any effort to meet up with him. Instead, he waited until Damon reached him.

He wasn't ready. '*God, I feel foolish,*' he thought to himself. This chump doesn't deserve my forgiveness. "*That's not what My Word says,*" he felt God guiding him.

"*You're right, I'm sorry, I need to humble myself, please fix my heart Jesus.*" As he silently prayed, peace and compassion overtook him. God had equipped him to forgive his brother. He wasn't ready to trust him just yet, maybe that'll come in time. For now, they will take it slow.

"Hi, David," Damon said, nodding his head as he called his name.

David lifted his head to nod a return greeting without speaking.

"Can we talk," Damon asked, hoping his brother was ready to let him back in his life?

"Sure, let's go out back," David said, moving through the crowded kitchen and out the sliding door to the back yard. Damon followed suit.

April noticed the men walking to the back yard. Deloris walked up to her with a hopeful look in her eye. Together they said a quick prayer that there would be peace between the brothers.

There was a picnic table next to the grill. David sat on the bench near the house, Damon sat across from him. Their parents had a lamp post next to the table and grill, so the two were able to look each other in the eye.

Damon spoke first. "David, I'm sorry…"

"Don't," David exclaimed! "Just listen." He took a deep breath before he began. "In all honesty and fairness, I've known Jackie was unhappy the whole time we were married. As a matter of fact, I begged her to marry me. I should have known then that it wasn't going to work. Not only that, everyone kept telling me that she wasn't into me, or she wasn't the one. Her own mother even told me I could have done better, but I didn't want to hear it. I just wished you all would have told me." David wasn't blind to Jackie's feelings, but it was difficult for him to accept the fact that he couldn't please her when that's all he wanted to do.

Damon didn't know what to say, he was stunned by David's admission. "Are you saying you're partly responsible for what we did," Damon asked? Bewilderment crowded his thoughts. What was David trying to say?

"I'm saying that if I had been honest with myself, a lot of things could have been avoided," he explained. David could see that his brother was puzzled. "Bottom line, if I'd taken my head out of the sand, maybe Jackie and I could have communicated better and worked out our problems."

"You've got to be kidding me," Damon interjected.

His brother interrupted him. "Don't get me wrong, I'm not condoning what you all did." David said, speaking to him like there had never been a rift between them.

"So... you don't want me to apologize," Damon asked? He squinted his eyes together trying to make sense of what David was saying.

They stared at each other for a minute and then broke out in laughter. Deloris, Joseph and April came running from the house toward the brothers. The two stood and embraced. Their mother cried tears of joy. Before they knew it, everyone was outside welcoming Damon back into the family. Everyone hugged and congratulated the twins for coming back together.

"I take it you two made up," Micki's remark was sarcastic as always.

"Yeah, lil sis, we did. What are you gonna do about it," David asked, teasing her to ease the tension she had against Damon?

She scoffed, "you clown," and playfully shoved him away.

Micki reluctantly hugged Damon, the relationship between the two had been strained, since they were children. His betrayal intensified it even more. However, if David could forgive so could she.

David looked at his future bride. A weight was lifted off his shoulders and he felt a peace he'd never experienced before that moment. He winked at her; his gaze gave her the assurance that all was well. David started walking toward the driveway.

"Where are you going," his mother asked?

"To see Jackie," he called out, as he continued to walk.

"What, why," Deloris questioned?

The rest of the family grumbled, also wanting to know the reason. She was the last person he needed to see.

Chris stopped him. "Dude, you just got engaged," he said. "Why are you going to see your ex-wife?"

"It's ok, April knows what I need to do," he said. "You can ask her, if you don't believe me."

He turned to look at his future sister-in-law. She nodded her head in agreement. Chris moved out of the way, so David could finish what he started.

Jackie was sitting at the dining room table with Bernice. Her cell phone rang. It was David. She hurriedly answered the call. He was on his way over. It happened; she had done it. But how? She hadn't shown him as much attention, as she wanted. Maybe he realized that he still loved her, when she left the house. Maybe April was not the woman of his dreams, after all.

Jackie sent her mother back home. Excited about what was about to take place, she quickly showered, changed into a pink summer casual t-shirt sundress. David always said she looked sexy in it. She sprayed cherry blossom body spray and covered her lips with a red watermelon flavored lip gloss. Her naturally curly hair was rough looking. She combed the nicer side and pinned the rougher side up. This was the first time in a long time that she was eager to see David. Life was starting to come together, or so it seemed.

The doorbell rang, and it was him. Jackie rushed to open the door. Once the door was opened, her excitement took a nose dive. David wasn't alone. Damon, the children, and April were with him.

The group was astonished at her appearance. She was dressed, like she was going on a date.

Damon asked her, "are you going somewhere?"

"Mommy, where are you going," Tony asked?

"Nowhere." She commented.

Damon was still joking with her. "Are you sure, because you didn't have that on at Mom and Dad's?"

"Shut up," she replied. Crestfallen, she stepped back to let everyone in. "Why are you here," she said with a bad attitude now?

Jackie was embarrassed that she had gotten it all wrong. Now they all knew what she was hoping and thinking. She harshly told the children to go to bed, and she didn't want to hear any noise.

"Well, that was mean," Damon scolded, going upstairs with the children.

"What do you want, David," Jackie asked again? She snapped at him and refused to look his way. He and April sat on the couch, which was in front of the window. Jackie sat across from them with her arms folded, legs crossed, and her face turned toward the wall.

David was reluctant to speak. It was obvious that she was expecting him to come solo. Her demeanor suggested that she was looking for a romantic night with him. He was shell shocked. There was no telling how April was feeling. He had put her in an uncomfortable position again. "I'm here to apologize," David explained.

Jackie looked up at the ceiling with her head still turned away. *What does that mean, she thought? Is he apologizing for making a fool of her, for bringing his fiancé to her home, what?* She finally looked at him. "What are you apologizing for," Jackie asked, with a defeated tone?

"For what I put you through," he explained, repeated to her a similar speech to the one that he gave Damon. He was sorry that he didn't take her feelings into consideration. It was all about him and what he wanted. No matter what she's done, he needed to focus on the things he could have done better in their marriage.

After he was done apologizing, the couple stood up. "That's all I wanted to say. I'm sorry you thought that it was something else. I hope that you understand that April will soon be my wife, so please don't mistake my willingness to speak as a sign that we're getting back together."

There were no words to express what she felt about what she had just heard. Jackie couldn't even formulate a sentence to describe what she was feeling. He put some of the blame on himself. Who does that? Her father never took blame for her mother's infidelity. Jackie realized that David had done some major self-reflection.

Damon came back down stairs. He looked where his brother had sat.

"They're gone. I'm surprised you didn't have your woman with you." The sadness in her voice was evident. She had lost both men.

"I can't believe you thought David wanted to get back with you," Damon said. "He's been deeply hurt, and even though he's being kind to us both, he's definitely not totally over it."

"Please do not tell anyone what just happened," Jackie implored. She already looked stupid in front of her family and didn't want people talking about her even more. "Yeah, I won't say anything," Damon agreed, before leaving the house.

Jackie didn't believe him. Once you are the laughing stock and the brunt of everyone 's joke, it starts to take a hold of you. She knew that she needed a new start, but where does she begin?

Chapter 21

By Sunday morning, David couldn't wait to attend service. He anticipated a good word from the bishop, as he has always delivered a blessed sermon. The household finished breakfast in time for the departure. Trina and April cooked pancakes, bacon, and scrambled eggs.

April was excited about going to service as well. This was something new for him to share a healthy, vibrant appreciation for the Lord. All the years they spent together, he hoped Jackie would change her mind and come to know Christ, but that never happened. All he could do now is continue to pray for her and believe God would capture her heart.

David's parents and future in-laws decided to meet at the church. April volunteered to drive, since he drove all day yesterday. She wanted him to enjoy his time visiting his family also. That was one of the many things he loved about her. His fiancée always thought about his wants and needs.

He laughed to himself, because he got giddy just thinking about April. At times, he acts like he's never been in love before. What he was most glad about was that April felt the same way about him. This was a new experience for both of them. It didn't matter who approved or disapproved of their relationship. They would soon be husband and wife.

The church's ministry had grown by leaps and bounds since he left. God was truly elevating this hub of hope. Praise and worship were on point, as the praise team ushered in the presence of God with singing and dancing. April raised her hands and sang along with the praise team.

After the praise team finished, the pastor brought forth the Word with power and conviction. The sermon encouraged the people to stand on the promises of God. He asked the congregation to remain steadfast, unmovable, and always abound in the work of the Lord. The portion of the sermon that really captured him was the part about divine delay. The pastor said that sometimes a blessing is delayed to allow an individual to learn a lesson or improve character. The church roared, with members shouting amen to the Word from the man of God.

After church, David wanted to continue the tour of Detroit with April and her family. This was their first time in Michigan, as well. As soon as the church service was over, they headed out. Everyone dressed down for Sunday service. April wanted David's parents to come, but everyone was expected back at the house for Sunday dinner.

April and her family admired the Campbell's for keeping that old tradition alive. On the menu today was lasagna, and apple pie for dessert. Even though her parents wanted to see downtown, they couldn't get enough of the Campbell family. They talked David into going back to his parents' home. April was glad because she believed that he was drained from yesterday.

Everyone returned to the parents' home. The family started a new thing. usually Deloris, Micki, and Trina would cook Sunday dinner. Since David left, it was switched off with the men. The women would cook one Sunday, the men would take the following Sunday, on the fifth Sunday, they would potluck. This Sunday, it was the ladies' turn.

All of the grown women occupied the kitchen. Deloris and Gladys took care of the lasagna. Everyone pitched in wherever needed. April worked on the salad. Micki and Trina got the plastic ware, paper plates and drinks together. The desserts were prepared the night before by April's mother and sisters.

The men were in the living room talking sports and waiting for the NBA playoff game. All of the children were scattered around the house. The younger children had to stay in the basement. The grandparents built a play area for them, since there were so many. The older children were either outside or upstairs. Damon and

Bridget even showed up. The two of them would watch the younger kids. Everyone was there except Jackie and her children.

April went to ask David about Junior and Nakita, as well as the other children. Just then, the doorbell rang. Jackie walked in with the children. The men gave each other puzzled looks, as she hadn't stayed for Sunday dinner in a long time.

Jackie started to make her way to David, but Joseph told her that the ladies were in the kitchen. It wasn't a harsh tone but firm. She stared at April before moving to the kitchen. April looked at David, who was seated next to her during the exchange between Joseph and Jackie. He placed his arm around her shoulders.

Deloris was shocked and disturbed to see Jackie walk into the kitchen. If the girl was here for a peaceful visit, the intrusion would be acceptable. The family hoped that Jackie didn't come to start any drama. They had to treat her kindly for the sake of the children.

Deloris pulled Jackie outside to the backyard and swung Jackie around toward the table. "Sit down," she instructed firmly!

Jackie was a little shaken. Her ex-mother-in-law hadn't been so hostile toward her in the past. She sat down on the bench.

"What are you doing here, Jackie," Deloris asked in exasperation?

"I'm here to see David, if that's ok." She refused to feel uncomfortable. If no one wanted her around, that was too bad for them.

Deloris shook her head. "Don't you come over here starting trouble. You hear," she warned

Jackie rose from her seat. "Why do you always think I'm trying to start something," she smiled, making her way back to the kitchen?

"Because I know you," Deloris explained. "You can play that innocent role with someone else." Deloris and the family have seen up close and personal the junk Jackie has done.

212

"Why are you being so mean," Jackie inquired? "David has forgiven me..."

"David has forgiven you, but David doesn't want you," Deloris explained, following Jackie. "There's a difference." She knew like everyone else what Jackie thought the night before. Damon told Deloris that she dressed up for a night out with David.

She scoffed. "I just need to ask him a question, and then I'll leave." Jackie walked towards the house. Deloris called out to her, but she kept going. She made it back inside the house, walked through the kitchen, and into the living room where the men were sitting.

Jackie sucked her teeth. "Can we speak," she asked, looking straight at David? April was next to him, with her arm looped possessively around his arm.

"There's nothing to talk about Jackie," he said bluntly. She doesn't back down easily. He was ready to go toe to toe with her, if it came to that.

She folded her arms. "I just need to ask you a question," Jackie said, getting perturbed. All she wanted to do was ask a simple question.

"Ok, send a text to my mom, and she'll relay the question to me," David offered the compromise, not believing she really needed to ask him anything, she was just trying to be nosy.

A frown appeared, and anger rose up within her. "You know what, since you're in the apologizing business, how about you take Dana with you to Georgia."

The family scoffed, murmured, and some even laughed. David thought about how he would respond. After the DNA test results came back, he might consider bringing Dana to Georgia, but this wasn't the time to discuss it. He told her so.

Jackie was livid. He required her to have all those babies, and now he wouldn't help her. They wanted to play hardball; she will play even harder. "You can bring the kids home, when you're ready." She stomped out of the house.

Chapter 22

Jackie's departure a few nights ago hadn't ruined the time he spent with his family. David had a great time, and it was bittersweet leaving the family in Michigan. The twins were staying for the summer. He and April split the return drive evenly. It was a blessing that his uncle picked up Aunt Gladys, once they arrived at David's home. She would have had to spend the night, because David was too tired to drive to Riverdale and head back up to Lilburn. He dropped April off first, and then headed home.

The house was serene without the twins. This alone time will allow him to rest. David reflected on the trip and his conversations with Damon and Jackie. He laughed to himself, as he thought about how far they had all come since he left Michigan to move to Georgia.

His mind shifted to April. She didn't want much, but he had every intention of giving her everything. David wondered, if she wanted her own babies. He'd spoken with her about bringing Tony and Ashley to visit some holidays, and she was open to it. Also, he will be responsible for three children instead of two. That didn't deter April either.

With all five of Jackie's children in Michigan, she would have her hands full. Damon would likely take Ashley and Tony, and his mother would help. However, he knew that some of Jackie's frustration stemmed from the fact that she simply needed a break from working and taking care of children all the time. He'd speak with his mother about how they could help her.

David stopped himself, realizing that he was still making plans for Jackie. He had a new wife-to-be to look after, and shifted his focus to April to concentrate on how he could make her life better before dropping off to sleep.

The next morning, April sat at her desk looking at an online wedding dress catalog. She couldn't believe she and David were tying the knot. Her first wedding was quick and small, but David said this one will be large and planned very well. They were both excited.

She thought about the conversation David had with Jackie, apologizing for his mistakes in the relationship. He knew she was miserable and didn't offer a way out. Relationships are always about loving and being loved. April loved the way David catered to her and showered her with gifts. She has never had it so good.

Clicking through the selection, April noticed a dress, which took her breath away. She'd always pictured herself walking down the aisle in something just like it. April was sure David would also love it. She called the shop to find out, if the dress was available in her size. The dress search turned out to be easier than she expected. April hoped the rest of the wedding planning would be so simple.

The next day, both David and April decided to take the day off from work to spend time together. David let April make the decision as to where they would go for the day. She chose an amusement park, and David felt that he couldn't have thought of anything better to do.

On Fridays, amusement parks are crowded, but it didn't matter to them. They were together and relishing the time spent with each other. Both were very fond of roller coasters, so they decided to ride every roller coaster they could before the end of the day.

The lovebirds walked hand in hand excited for what the future would bring. They reached the first coaster, which spins riders upside down. The line was long as expected, about an hour wait. As they waited to ride, David and April quizzed each other on how much of the Turkish language they knew, as they both studied it diligently. The exchange was so delightful that it helped time pass. They made it to the platform quickly. As a thrill seeker, David wanted the front seat, and April reluctantly agreed.

April was nervous, she's ridden this ride several times but never in the front. As the coaster slowly made its way to the top, she silently prayed. Her hands started sweating. They were at the top, and she heard David say, "here we go." As the coaster rolled down the hill, April's stomach dropped. She screamed, as it was scary seeing the track as the ride moved quickly. Normally she closed her eyes, as the train made its descent. This time she kept them open, holding tightly to David's hand. The initial drop is the hardest to experience. After the ride was over, the adrenaline pumped even more.

David teased April, because of the scream on the ride. She laughed as he continued to kid around. They came to the second ride. This was a wooden coaster. The line wasn't as long as the first ride. They rode up front again, this time April would close her eyes so that she won't feel the drop as the ride slides down the hill.

At the end of the day, the couple walked back to David's truck, singing praise and worship songs. On the way home, they kept talking about the day and how much fun they had. As David stood at April's door, he placed his arms around her waist. April held his gaze, wrapping her arms around his neck. "This is the most fun I've had at an amusement park in a long time," she interjected. "I've never laughed so hard."

David planted a kiss on her lips. "Thank you for being a generous sport."

April laughed, "what does that mean actually?"

"You didn't cock an attitude, when I asked you to ride up front and you did it for all the rides." He found himself silently comparing April to Jackie, because Jackie got mad whenever he suggested it.

"Oh, well I trust your judgment, even though that first ride was way scarier than I imagined," she said. She really enjoyed riding in the front, especially with the love of her life. "We definitely have to do this again."

"I'm sure we will," David replied. "I can't wait." Placing a soft kiss on her forehead, David heard April sigh softly. He kissed her lips and released her to go into her unit. April opened the door, and David waited until she came back to signal that the coast was clear, before he left for home.

Four months later...

Georgia

April's heart skips a beat as she thinks of David, a man who supports her decisions and cares for her deeply. She, her mother, and sisters were going to pick up their dresses and run errands for the wedding. Her sister Keisha insisted on making something for the wedding. They wouldn't allow her to cook, so she chose a decoration.

David wanted to pay for everything. Usually, the bride's family paid, but he wanted to give her everything she wanted. Even though April's parents are well off, he insisted that it be his bill.

The bridesmaids were her three sisters, with Saxin as the matron of honor. The groomsmen were Damon, Junior, and Chris. They expected all of David's nieces, nephews, some cousins, and friends to attend. They're all due to arrive on Thursday evening for the wedding on Saturday.

There were about 500 responses to the invitations between both families, church family, coworkers, and friends. The hall was large enough to hold 1,500 people. David wanted to make sure there was room enough to dance. He also wanted something different at the reception, a play area for the children. That way, parents didn't have to leave the reception area to check on their kids.

The reception hall was huge. The space is big enough for a large dance floor and for everyone to maneuver and have a bouncy house for the kiddos. April couldn't hold back from smiling. The owner met with them and showed her the paperwork, where David signed for the venue and paid the rental fee in full. Everything was in order.

April sent David a message letting him know how the day went. She promised to call him, when she arrived at home.

After saying goodbye to April, a video call came to David's tablet. He thought it was April again. As he accepted the call, he realized that it was Bernice. "Hi Bernice," he said. It wasn't a joyful greeting.

"David, it's so good to see you. You didn't come see me the last time you were home." Bernice just went on talking, explaining that she knew he was busy and only came to retrieve his children. "So, I hear the wedding is this Saturday," she continued.

So that was it, she called about the wedding, David thought. *She was looking for an invitation; not going to happen. After all the drama she tried to cause when she first met April, there was no way in the world this woman will attend this blessed event.* "Yes, it is, I'm very excited," he responded.

"You didn't want to invite your old mother-in-law," Bernice said grinning. As always, she was up to something.

"That would be inappropriate Bernice," David replied. Certainly, she knew that he couldn't invite her.

"Well, what about the children. I haven't seen them since before you came for them." David purposely didn't take the children to see her. She would have begged him to move back home. "Aren't you going on a honeymoon," Bernice asked?

"Yes, we're going on a Caribbean cruise for a week; then we'll go on a Hawaiian cruise right after."

"Two-week honeymoon?" She was silent for a bit; he and Jackie only had a one-week honeymoon to Disney World. "Well, who's going to watch the children while you're gone," she inquired?

David chuckled. "My parents are staying the two weeks we will be gone," he said. He made the arrangements back in August. The children are excited to spend time with their grandparents.

Bernice sighed; she should have known arrangements were already made. Truth was, she was lonely. Jackie was gone, and her two sons are still bitter from her adulterous affair decades ago. Jada only came around when she wanted something.

The Campbell family stayed together even in the midst of betrayal. David forgave his brother and they're back on speaking terms. Why isn't her family like that? Charles told her she would die a lonely old woman for what she had done. He hasn't found it in his heart to forgive her either.

David could see that Bernice was troubled. Compassion came upon him for his ex-mother-in-law. Bernice was a little selfish at times, but she meant well. He knew all too well that she's been abandoned by her family and friends. His family was the only family she had. He won't invite her to the wedding, but she can come see the children.

"How about you come see the children," he offered. "I'll let my parents know. What do you say?" His parents will probably fuss at him for inviting her, but the three of them can take care of the children together.

"Are you serious," she gushed? "I can come." Her face lit up like a Christmas tree at the invite.

"You can come to the house, but not the wedding or reception." He probably will regret his decision. If she tries anything beforehand, he'll have her removed at once.

"That's ok by me, I'll be with all my grandchildren," Bernice said excitedly. She thanked David then hung up.

David thought about what he just did. He didn't feel comfortable leaving her alone like that. What would Jesus do? He would have extended an invitation as well. Love like Jesus, is what his pastor always says. He called April and his parents to give them the news.

Family and friends started arriving Thursday afternoon. All of the Campbell's came in Thursday evening. The twins and Dana were ecstatic. The whole family was attending the wedding. They will get to see everyone except their mother. No one knew where she was.

Bernice was welcomed by the family. Everyone was aware that she will always be around because of her grandchildren. Jackie had taken off on a vacation, because she didn't want to be around for the wedding. If Jackie were still around, Bernice wouldn't be in Georgia.

To David's surprise, April didn't mind Bernice attending the wedding. He was relieved that she was so understanding about Bernice's last-minute invitation to participate in the weekend, if not the wedding festivities.

Friday, the day before the wedding was hectic for everyone. The brothers had to get their tuxedos, and the women wanted to get their hair and nails done. All of David's female relatives refused to get beautified at home. They were afraid the style wouldn't hold. Some of them had to get last minute items like shoes and makeup. Everyone looked stunning at the dress rehearsal, then took off to dinner at a steakhouse in Buckhead.

When the wedding day arrived, a clear sunny day with a light breeze met the participants. April remembered her parents telling her that if she married on a sunny day, the marriage would last long. She didn't know how true it was, but she was happy for a sunny day.

The traditional something old, something new, something borrowed, and something blue was presented to her after taking pictures. Her mother gave her earrings that she had since Keisha was born, the new was the pearl earrings she wore with her dress. Deloris gave her a pearl necklace to wear with the earrings, and she wore a blue garter belt.

It was four o'clock, time for the wedding to begin. David was at the altar with his best man Damon. The other groomsmen walked down the aisle with the bridesmaids. The maid of honor Saxin walked by herself. As the bridal party walked down the aisle, April's cousin Raymond sang Stevie Wonder's song, *A Ribbon in The Sky*. Chris and Tonya started down the aisle first. The groomsmen were adorned in black tuxedos with white shirts and royal blue cummerbunds. David wore the same with a tail jacket.

Saxin walked in right on cue. The flower girl and ring bearer came next, the two walked together with big grins on their faces. Some of the guests started laughing. The flowers were blue and yellow in color. Aisha dropped the flowers as instructed, a flower on each side of her as she walked. The flower girl's dress was white in color, illusion cap sleeves, embellished bodice and satin beaded belt. The ring bearer wore a tux just like the groomsmen.

The doors closed, as Raymond finished the song right on time. It was David's turn to serenade April, while she walked down the aisle. He sang her favorite love song, *You and I* by O'Bryan. As soon as the doors opened, April and her dad William appeared. The audience stood and David began singing. His baritone voice permeated the room, uplifting the guests and touching April's heart. The bride and father stood a few inches from the alter arm in arm, as David finished singing. They waited until the minister asked the question, who gives this woman away?

William spoke up and handed April over to David. Bishop Hutchins began, "dearly beloved we gather today to join this man and this woman in holy matrimony."

As the pastor continued to speak, those closest to April and David started shedding tears. They both had suffered infidelity from their previous partners. It was a miracle that God helped them find one another.

"Let us pray," Bishop Hutchins said. The congregation bowed their heads. The bishop led the prayer for David and April to have a loving, long-standing, joyful marriage throughout their days and to let no man put asunder whom He has joined together. "In the mighty name of Jesus we pray, Amen," the bishop prayed. The wedding guests all said amen in unison.

He asked a question to the groom. "David, do you take April to be your lawfully wedded wife and to live in holy matrimony? Will you love, honor, comfort, and cherish her from this day forward, forsaking all others, for as long as you both shall live?"

David responded, "I do."

He asked April the same question. She responded with, "I do."

The pastor instructed the couple to face each other, hold hands, and repeat after him for the marriage vows. "I, David, take April to be my wedded wife, to have and to hold from this day forward, to love, honor and cherish." April repeated the same vows.

David looked deep into April's eyes, as he placed the ring on her finger. She blushed, as she placed a ring on David's finger, repeating the vow. "With this ring, I thee wed," the couple said to one another.

Bishop Hutchins said a few more words wishing them a loving journey and led another prayer thanking God for this union. "By the authority vested in me by the State of Georgia, I now pronounce you both husband and wife. You may now kiss your bride!"

David and April came together, locking lips for several seconds. The attendees erupted in cheers, when they pulled apart. The couple turned to face their guests.

The wedding celebration moved to the reception hall. The wedding party, parents, and children rode in two stretch limousines. Both were white in color with a stainless-steel bar, cup holders, ice bins, champagne buckets, overlay carpet, wood surfaces and chrome wheels.

Guests were amazed at the wedding hall's extravagant beauty. It was adorned in crystal chandeliers and mirrors, providing more than enough space for the dance floor, and offered a serving area and kids zone. The wedding party sat on the stage. A long, white tablecloth with a royal blue border covered their table. David and April sat in the middle. The bridesmaids were seated at April's right and the groomsmen at David's left.

The closest relatives had assigned tables, while everyone else sat where space was available. The tables were round with either white or blue cloths. The center pieces were opposite in color to accentuate the design. Keisha out did herself. The centerpieces sat on a mirror, the tall slender vases matched the wedding colors, they held either white marble or blue marble pieces. Each table had four sparkling beverage bottles. Alcoholic beverages were not allowed.

A decadent dinner menu included prime rib, baked chicken, combination potatoes and green beans, yams, fried corn, macaroni salad, pasta salad, salad, dinner rolls, and cornbread. Water and juice were also available to drink. The red, candy bar was opened, but children had to be accompanied by an adult.

Everyone ate to their heart's content. Every now and then someone would tap on a glass for the couple to share a kiss. April giggled at the constant chimes from guests tapping the crystal glasses. David just smiled, leaning over to kiss his new bride.

The wedding guests listened to a mixture of gospel, jazz, and old-school rhythm and blues. The couple wanted to start the dancing with the electric slide using Stevie Wonder's song, *My Eyes Don't Cry.*

David and April slow danced at the family's request. Afterward, guests packed the dance floor, line dancing to music. The disc jockey played a variety of group dancing music, prompting the dancers to perform the wobble, cupid shuffle, and cha-cha slide.

The hour was getting late, and they'd only rented the space for six hours. Midnight was the cut off time. At 11 o'clock, the cleanup crew started clearing the tables. Family helped pack and tote the many gifts that were on the gift table. Saxin kept the money pouch filled with gifts for the couple.

It was well after midnight, when David and April finished bringing all the gifts home. They gave his parents and Bernice instructions for the children, the house, and the vehicles. David left a substantial amount of cash for them. For the two weeks they'd honeymoon, David wanted to make sure his parents and Bernice had everything they needed to take care of Dana and the twins.

The couple changed clothes at home, said their goodbyes to everyone, and then headed to the hotel by the airport. They were catching a morning plane to Miami, Florida. After the landing, they'd go straight to the loading dock for a week-long Caribbean cruise.

At the hotel, David had reserved the newlywed suite. As they stepped inside their room, rose petals were all over the floor. The front room had a couch, bar, kitchen area, and table. A heart shape of rose petals covered the bed. David offered April a piece of fruit from the fruit basket on the dresser, as he opened a bottle of sparkling apple cider. April was overjoyed. David outdid himself. Everything was so elegant, well planned, and pleasing.

"David, I'm so elated," April gushed. "I couldn't have imagined anything nicer."

"Oh, that's nothing, wait until we're on the deck, watching the ships pass by and maybe even some dolphins jumping out of the water," he said. Placing the champagne glasses on the table, he reached out his hand toward April. She willingly walked into his arms.

Epilogue

April and David explored the Caribbean and Hawaii on their honeymoon, enjoying every minute.

Jackie followed Gladys' advice and began praying early every morning before work. She also found love in a new relationship.

The Campbell family welcomed Bernice to fellowship whenever they gathered. She was so overwhelmed by the family's love toward her that she accepted Christ as her savior.

Damon and Bridget married shortly after David and April. Together they are raising Dominique and co-parenting Tony and Ashley with Jackie. Damon received a promotion on the job, and his dinner sales are doing well. David is coaching them on how to handle their finances.

Although David and April experienced challenging first marriages, the couple fully appreciates each other. They pray and communicate to overcome differences, enjoying a joyous life together.

Fortunately, God can mend broken hearts.

Made in the USA
Columbia, SC
23 December 2021

50987235R00124